The World According to
Mimi Smartypants

The World According to Mimi Smartypants

Mimi Smartypants

AVON
TRADE

An Imprint of HarperCollins*Publishers*

FIRST EDITION

Interior text designed by Elizabeth M. Glover

Library of Congress Cataloging-in-Publication Data

Smartypants, Mimi.
    The world according to Mimi Smartypants / by Mimi Smartypants.—1st ed.
        p. cm.
ISBN-13: 978-0-06-078636-6 (acid-free paper)
ISBN-10: 0-06-078636-1 (acid-free paper)
1. Married women—Fiction. 2. Female friendship—Fiction. 3. Women cat owners—Fiction. 4. Chicago (Ill.)—Fiction.   I. Title.

PS3619.M37W67 2006
813'.6—dc22   2005016560

06 07 08 09 10 JTC/RRD 10 9 8 7 6 5 4 3 2 1

Dedicated to, and with appreciation for,
the City of Chicago and all the friends,
family, and total strangers within it
who help make my life completely ridiculous.

How do you start something like this? There is a huge temptation to get all Holden Caufield and reject the notion of autobiographical beginnings while simultaneously and sneakily giving an autobiographical beginning. Or we could be flirtatiously postmodern and talk about the book you are right now holding in your hands, book *qua* book—no, that's horrible. The most literary and novelistic thing would be to have some witty and revealing Prepackaged Character Sketch all at the ready, so you could tell within a few pithy sentences just what sort of narrator you will be dealing with here. I seem to be fresh out of those, however.

I don't even know precisely what "this" is. All I know is that once I turned thirty it seemed that I no longer knew what the rules were, was no longer sure of my attitudes toward anything, and no longer felt as if I had all the time in the world to decide how to live. Not to worry, this is not going to be some standard landing-a-man, starring-Meg-Ryan, dumb-ass romance story (I am married). Nor will it be plucky-career-girl-climbs-to-the-top (I am not at the top, exactly, but I am gainfully employed in the publishing field). I turned thirty, and I started keeping a diary. Not some sort of every-single-day "Dear Diary" thing, but just a way to capture this odd time in my life, when I am unequivocally an adult but not quite feeling like one. When I own a home and have a pension plan, but I still go out to punk rock shows and, through some primeval instinct held over from the student days, drink too much of the cheapest possible beer. When I have a job that I love, that pays me well and promotes me often, but I still break out in a rash when people refer to it a "career." I wrote this diary on my morning commute, as the El train rattled past the tired faces of Chicago buildings, all the fire escapes like crooked teeth. I wrote it at work, when I was supposed to be working. Sometimes I wrote it at home, after much wine-with-dinner. If you are hopelessly nosy and curious like I am, you might want to read it.

Definitely the most adult thing my husband LT and I have done yet was buying our condo. Getting married was a piece of cake compared with all the frightening mortgage-speak, the signing on the dotted line, and the vague freaked-out feeling that ohmygod I don't even know what I am doing next *week*, and I just took out a thirty-year loan? I am very happy in the new place, not least because the old one was so very small. I don't care how much in love you are with your spouse, there are going to be those moments when you think, *My god, you are always here.*

THINGS I LOVE ABOUT MY NEIGHBORHOOD

1. There are these benches, at least one on every block and sometimes more, that exist solely as parking places for old people. In nice weather each bench is overflowing with the elderly, and those who did not get there early enough to snag bench space sometimes bring milk crates or lawn chairs or other auxiliary hanging-out equipment. The benches are not segregated by ethnicity but by gender, alternating babushkas and stooped-over old men (sometimes with chessboards). I also should point out that these are not bus stops, they are not in green park-type areas but right up against the street, and no other neighborhood in

Chicago, to my knowledge, has these no-purpose benches. It is specific to Devon Avenue.

2. I can walk to amazing Indian food, wonderful sushi, and a twenty-four-hour diner. Down the street there is an Uzbekistani restaurant. The urge for Uzbek food has not yet struck, partially because I have no idea what Uzbeks eat, but there it is. There are also lots of kosher bakeries, which make the whole neighborhood smell like cinnamon sugar. Mmmmm.

3. Speaking of cinnamon, there is a synagogue less than a block from me that has a spiral-shaped roof. I think the builders meant for it to look like a Torah scroll, but to me it looks like a giant cinnamon bun, so I call it the Cinnamon-a-Gogue, which is very fun to say and makes me happy. Also, the end of my street features a giant light-up menorah, making it incredibly easy to give directions ("turn left at the giant menorah").

4. Watching the teenage Orthodox boys, in their black hats and suits, give each other soul-brother handshakes when they meet on the street.

5. The store called Islamic Books and Things, which is right next to a Russian bookstore, which is right next to a kosher bakery, which is right next to a Pakistani butcher shop, which is right next to an Indian candy store.

THINGS I DON'T LIKE SO MUCH ABOUT MY NEIGHBORHOOD

1. It is filthy. Much filthier than the rest of Chicago. Our streets are rarely cleaned and there is a lot of garbage and debris on the sidewalks.

2. The drugstore a few blocks away, which is a special circle of hell Dante must have forgotten to mention. Never think you are going to pop into this drugstore for "a few things" because you will be there the rest of your life. I know you think I'm exaggerating, but trust me.

3. The #155 bus does not run twenty-four hours, although it definitely should.

4. An overabundance of small children, especially in the summer. They like to play this game called "Run Around and Scream a Lot." I think they are really into historical reenactments, only instead of the usual Civil War battles, they focus on free-for-alls like the Attica prison uprising or the Watts riots.

5. I don't drive, so this doesn't really affect me much, but traffic on Devon is atrocious, particularly on the weekends.

⟵ July 8

It's time for every lazy diarist's favorite type of entry:

RANDOM FACTS!

Age: 30

Height: 5′1″

Weight: I never weigh myself, nor do I pay attention at the doctor's office. It says 127 pounds on my driver's license, that's probably about right.

I have dark brown hair and eyes that are the same color as the dark brown M&M's. Of course now that they got rid of the tan M&M's, the only brown is the dark brown.

I'm left-handed. I can do very little with my right hand.

I skipped a grade in grade school, due to my freakish reading abilities. I skipped second grade, if you must know.

Speaking of freakish reading abilities, I read at least two books for pleasure every week. Irritating quirk: even if I despise a book, I must read it until the end.

More quirks: I always look in other people's medicine cabinets when I get the chance. (Don't let me use the bathroom in your house.)

Yet more quirks! I intensely dislike: anyone touching my feet, the feel of a bare mattress, and sticking my hand inside an opaque bag (e.g., potato chips must be dumped out in a bowl or on a napkin). I know, I'm nuts.

Oh, and I also hate it when people say "ATM machine," since the "M" means "machine."

I started playing violin when I was very small, as one of those little-bespectacled-robot prodigies. Then I stopped for a while, after college, due to a bad case of musical burnout, and just recently I started taking lessons again.

I have never had a cavity.

I have one sister who's eight years younger than me. She's pretty cool.

I have had only three pets in my life: a parakeet when I was seven, my childhood dog who lasted seventeen years, and my current big fat floppy cat, named The Cat.

I lived in the Middle East for a year when LT had a Fulbright fellowship.

In college I double-majored in literature and ancient Greek.

I've taken a fair amount of hallucinogens, but don't anymore.

These days I stick mostly to beer or vodka cosmopolitans if I'm feeling girly.

I am a vegetarian, but not the kind who will hand you a pamphlet. Eat whatever you like and allow me to do the same, thanks.

I collect "housewife" and etiquette books from the 1930s and 1940s, odd consumer packaging, zines, and any record relating to dance crazes or with the word "hi-fi" in the title.

In high school I was quite goth and spent oodles of time on my eye makeup and getting my black black hair to hang over my eye just so. Occasionally I still like to dress up in twirly dresses and make like the undead at Neo's goth night.

You know what? I think that's enough with the random facts. More substantive entries will follow later. Now I have to go brush my teeth, because I don't want to break my no-cavities streak.

⟵ July 9

Did you know that the slogan for the Chicago Transit Authority is "Take It"? It's not a very good slogan, but at least its imperative mood is appropriate. It would be even more appropriate if "Take It" were bracketed by the following two phrases, in order:

1. "Bend Over and"
2. "Up the Ass."

I had to run errands yesterday and thus needed a different bus home, and that particular bus seems to be sort of a Loch Ness bus or a Sasquatch bus, in that there are many rumors and legends afoot, and everyone knows at least one person who claims to have seen this bus or even actually to have taken this bus somewhere, but there is precious little direct evidence that the bus exists. After waiting forever I instead traveled a meandering and convoluted route home, which sucked. Take it, indeed.

⟵July 10

A few days ago I was getting off the bus, and an extremely large man was huffing and puffing across the street, waving his arms and screaming something unintelligible as the bus pulled away. I felt that this was none of my concern. Until, that is, he planted his sweaty carcass in my path and roared, between his strangled incipient-cardiac-event gasps, "God, do you speak fucking English? I said *Hold the bus!*"

I am sick and tired of people asking me if I speak (fucking) English, a question I find incredibly insulting on so many levels. (Hey, guess what, moron, not everybody does, and even if they don't it is no reason to be rude. Also I would venture that I probably speak better English than you, and thanks so much for outing yourself as a racist jerk, since if you would say such a thing to a somewhat olive-toned white girl I don't even want to know what you say to people who actually are from other countries.)

Also, how exactly am I supposed to "hold the bus"? Use my Wonder Woman grappling hook to keep it in place?

Anyway, I had this gigantic sweat-panted man breathing on me and demanding to know if I speak English and why

I have failed in my bus-holding duties. This made me crabby and I snapped back, "Just wanted to see you try to run across the street, fat-ass." Then the light changed and I got on the train and felt horrible all the way from the Belmont stop to Damen because that was a cheap shot and I should not have said it. He totally started it but that is no excuse, and I resolved to try and keep my mouth shut more and not add to the petty verbal ugliness of the world, even when it comes in the form of a sweaty mean jerk who mysteriously blames me for missing the bus.

There is a skill that most of us city mice have. I call it the Urban Eye Slide. This is the ability to scope out one's surroundings quickly but without actually seeming to look at anything at all. This allows you to find the open seat on a crowded train, to move to the other side of the sidewalk well in advance of people handing out flyers or crappy free newspapers, or to sort of let your eyes skip over the spare-changing homeless guy on the corner, while pasting what you hope is a small wistful sympathetic smile on your face. However, the Urban Eye Slide has its drawbacks. I have stood on El platforms right next to people I actually know and not seen them. Also, sometimes the practice of Urban Eye Slide will result in you missing out on really great crazy-person chatter. When I got on the train yesterday morning a casual glance around revealed an open seat next to a wild-haired woman who was muttering to herself in that cartoony crazy-person way, the way where you actually turn your head back and forth as if there are invisible people on either side of you. I took a seat behind her instead, playing it safe, but instantly regretted that when I kept overhearing snippets of her high-quality crazy material, such as "Those aren't stars on the American flag, they're *teeth*!" All the way downtown I leaned forward, straining to hear, notebook at the ready, but everything else was too garbled and quiet.

Strangely popular this week. Dinner or bar dates almost every night, which is fun, but sometimes I long for a plain old nesting night with LT. Last night I went with Rebecca to a little BYOB Italian place. Showing up with a surprisingly excellent eight-dollar bottle of Côtes du Rhône rather than paying restaurant markup is great for the wallet. However, having to work right next to a bottle of wine all day, while you impatiently wait for five o'clock, is bad for the nerves.

⟵ July 11

Kat and I went out on Thursday and stayed out too late (I swear to god the hours between eight and midnight *do not exist* at the Goldstar Bar). For a while we talked to some University of Chicago law school student. I was wearing a shirt with a strange distorted near-plaid pattern on it, and one of the first things this guy said to me was "You look like an Art Deco lumberjack." I think this is just about the best compliment ever.

⟵ July 12

I have never been able to live with someone for more than ten weeks. Except for LT, and he is tougher than most.

Sometimes there would be spectacular endings to the roommate situation, with recriminations and silent treatments. Sometimes things just fizzled out, or a better living situation would present itself. Sometimes it was my fault, sometimes it was hers. One way or another, I learned very quickly that it's better for everyone if I live by myself.

Let me just say by way of disclaimer that I hold no animosity whatsoever toward any of these former housemates. I mean, what's the consistent factor here? Me. It stands to reason that I am the one who is difficult to live with. Also, any annoying habits these people once had have probably faded with maturity (I think we're all less annoying now than we were eight years ago, wouldn't you agree?).

1. My first roommate, the one I was randomly matched with freshman year of college (the school claimed they carefully matched up personalities but I do not see how that can be true), was a very tall athletic blond we'll call Diane. Just standing next to her made me feel like a hunchbacked barefoot Gypsy girl. She was from West Virginia, her father was a prominent judge, she played the harp, she was on the tennis team, and she had always attended private girls-only boarding schools. She claimed to be an atheist but had a moral code stricter than any Mormon's, and I continually seemed to be shocking her without half trying. There was nothing wrong with Diane, but our neuroses did not mesh well. Eventually all the stress and strain manifested itself in a blowup over something quite minor; I promptly offered to be the one to move out, into a tiny single room. Sweet, blessed solitude.

2. Next, I attempted to live with a friend. Outwardly, this seemed to make more sense. We had similar taste in music, we both smoked, we had similar politics and fashion sense. (In college those two things go together more often than they should. Hip hip hooray for identity politics.) However, she turned out to be one of those girls who is perpetually having an emotional crisis/anxiety attack/weeping spell and needs the current man in her life to rescue her from that. *It gets old, people.* Also, since I am inner-directed to the point of autism, there was a definite clash of personalities and cultures. She soon moved out to be with Rescuing Boy full-time, and I had the place to myself.

3. Then there was a similar, very brief attempt to live with another friend. Apparently I continually annoyed her but she never saw fit to tell me so, until one Night of Great Drama, *Who's Afraid of Virginia Woolf?*–style, where all the passive aggressiveness came to a head and it was revealed that she had made plans to move out. So again I got the place to myself. Not a problem.

4. This one doesn't quite belong here, because it was a success story, but it was again a very brief roommate situation. One summer when I stayed on campus to fulfill some pseudo-bohemian fantasy of mine (I worked on a small literary magazine, oooh how indie), I lived in a cooperative house and roomed with this girl who was there to work on an honors project. We actually got along great (and still do), but the whole rest of the house used to joke about how different we were. Laura had a bed, a proper piece of furniture, whereas I slept (or passed out, usually) on a nonfoldout couch covered in an old quilt. Laura was up with the sun nearly every morning, making hearty farm-girl breakfasts in our tiny kitchen. "Want some?" she would ask me, to which I'd always answer "God, no," as I struggled up to a sitting position, pulled on my silk kimono, and lit the first cigarette of the day, leftover eyeliner pooled around my sockets like some low-budget Courtney Love. Laura now has two small sons and is still a smart cookie. I'm a little in awe of her.

From then on, I lived alone, until LT and I moved in together. A few years ago Kat stayed with us for a month, while she looked for a new apartment, and that went surprisingly well; we are both very personal-space-oriented and thus alternated between giggling on the couch with beer and disappearing completely for hours.

←—*July 13*

At work, a woman gets on the elevator and pushes a button, then gasps, "Oh my god!" and pushes a different button. She turns and looks directly at me with these big Stricken Hurt-Animal Eyes of Great Pleadingness. "I am so sorry," she says. "I pushed the wrong button!" "It's okay," I say, and stare off in the middle distance with my special This Conversation Is Over posture. She tries to laugh but it comes out shaky and weird. "Now we're going to have to stop! Sorry! Oh well." The elevator stops at the floor neither of us want and she jabs at the Close Door button a million fucking times, saying, "Sorry." I fully expected her to start punching herself in the head and saying, "Stupid! Stupid! stupid!" like a retarded kid in an afterschool special.

Elevator Lady? Listen carefully. The medication is not working.

◄—July 14

AM I STUPID OR AM I SMART?

Stupid: I once ran full-tilt face-first into a tree, cartoon-style, while tripping on mushrooms.

Smart: I did not go to graduate school. Graduate school was something I had once considered, until I realized I was only considering it because I couldn't think of anything else to do.

Stupid: I had an opportunity once to learn a new skill and take on a new responsibility at work, and I turned it down because it sounded boring. It turns out it *is* boring, horrendously boring, but it is also very highly paid, so I probably should have put up with it for a little while at least.

Smart: Buying my condo instead of waffling about it and continuing to rent.

Stupid: All the times I hopped on the El when we lived in Hyde Park, because it was right there and convenient, and not remembering that the Red Line drops one's puny tipsy white-girl ass off at Fifty-fifth and the expressway, which is not the most welcoming neighborhood in which to be waiting for a bus at night. It's perfectly fine during the day but one should spring for a cab in the evenings.

Smart: Dropping calculus at the last possible second and switching to a required math class that didn't make me cry on a daily basis.

Stupid: Eating chocolate-covered coffee beans and drinking coffee at the same time, while I was working on a paper. Worst caffeine psychosis ever. At one point I actually believed I had grown wings, that my skin had become transparent, and that my mystical babblings about modernist literary criticism made any sense at all.

Smart: Sneaking out the back door when the cops showed up. It's a long story.

— July 16

WATCH OUT! IT'S THE THEY PEOPLE!

I did not change my name when I got married. A lot of it was pure laziness—I simply couldn't deal with the effort it would take to change over my passport, utility bills, magazine subscriptions, yadda yadda. And I already had a box of five hundred business cards, and my name on an office door. There were also philosophical problems: why does being married mean you have to have the same name? If anyone can make a good argument for the necessity of it I will listen, but I doubt that you can. Anyway, I was discussing this fact with an older woman at work, who has a daughter who will get married next weekend, and she was all perplexed to find that I did not have a married name, and she asked, "Didn't they change it for you?" Who are "they"? I said, "Uhh . . . no" and we left it at that.

My freshman year in college, I always took a certain route back to my dorm from the library or dining hall, a route that took you through a kind of wooded area. One day there was a dead bird lying on the ground. I got sort of used to seeing the dead bird and watching the progress of its decay every evening after dinner. In fact, as a friendly gesture toward the dead bird's spirit, I began to yell, "Dead Bird!" every time I passed it. (Also, when you have obsessive-compulsive tendencies, things that are amusing one time quickly become rituals.) So life went on, and I saw the dead bird every day for about a month. One day, mysteriously, it was gone. Just gone. I went to yell my customary "Dead Bird!" but there was no dead bird. For a while I thought about yelling "Inexplicable Absence of Dead Bird!" every time I passed, but that just seemed too cumbersome and I gave up.

═══ *July 20*

THE TIME I HALLUCINATED AN ENTIRE RESTAURANT

A few years ago, I was walking back to my office from lunch. Lunchtime options are plentiful near my building, which is just north of the Chicago River and near all the high-end shopping and other tourist traps, but it is always nice to see new restaurants. As I strolled past the corner of Wabash and Huron, I was pleased to see, in place of the dry cleaner's that had been there, an empty storefront with a sign that said COMING SOON: NORTH AFRICAN FOOD AND COUS-COUS. Hmm, I thought. That could be pleasant. I pictured myself getting veg couscous takeout, or even better, some Ethiopian dish with that delightful spongy bread. About two weeks later, I thought, Hey, that couscous place should be open by now, and I walked back to that storefront, only to find the dry cleaner's right where it always had been and no couscous restaurant in sight. I even walked around, several blocks in each direction, just to make sure I hadn't misremembered the location. No couscous restaurant. Anywhere.

Scary. But it would have been even scarier if I had actually *had lunch* at the imaginary restaurant. Then I would have checked myself in for a rest cure.

⟵ *July 21*

Still kind of sleepy and out of sorts. Saucer-eyed and dreamy-brained. I feel like throwing myself on the mercy of the world. I went to a meeting yesterday, and I was early. (Note: I am always early, for everything. It's a sickness, and it seems to be getting worse with age. Eventually I'll start arriving for things a day or so in advance and will have to be put up in a guest room.) Someone else arrived early as well, and she and I were chatting about water intake, and she mentioned that she had a susceptibility to getting dehydrated and felt dizzy if she didn't drink enough liquid. I said, "Me too! If I'm not constantly drinking I just don't feel right." You already guessed it; the majority of the other attendees arrived just as I made that "constantly drinking" comment. Fantastic for my career, I'm sure.

 *July 22*

WAYS IN WHICH I AM LIKE EITHER AN ELDERLY PERSON OR A TINY CHILD

1. Sometimes, when I am hanging out reading or watching television, I will have my hand down my pants. I'm not *doing* anything, mind you. It just feels right.

2. I take naps. In fact, I *need* to take a nap on Sundays or I start to get cranky and whiny.

3. I get in food ruts: for days at a time I will want to eat only candy or oatmeal or tofu hot dogs or grapes or peanut butter and jelly sandwiches or oshinko maki.

4. Sometimes people don't understand what I say. I don't know if I slur my words, have an actual speech impediment, or just talk fast.

5. I almost always use two hands when drinking hot beverages.

6. I repeatedly implore my friends to go play bingo with me. (So far, no takers.) Doesn't that sound like fun? *Bingo!* Coffee and doughnuts! Fabulous prizes! So much better than that lame-o karaoke all the kids are into nowadays.

← July 23

It is a cranky day. The universe is very anti-Mimi. First, I got sniped at about something at work that was not really my fault, and isn't that just a joy with performance reviews coming up soon. Instead of a raise or a bonus, I will probably get a plate of cold leftover macaroni and a hearty handshake. I was also all proud that I seem to have mostly gotten over my cold, except for a touch of the Sultry Frog voice, when this afternoon I was seized with a coughing fit that was like something a pack-a-day Kentucky coal miner might have near the end of his life, and of course helpful coworkers came over to offer assistance while my eyes watered and my face turned pale with hectic Raggedy Ann cheeks and I made all kinds of unladylike wheezing noises. Get a clue, it does not do any good to hang around my office saying, "Are you okay?" repeatedly like a moron while I choke and sputter; just let me get this chunk of lung up and I will be fine.

← July 25

Yesterday was a Power Suit day. I had lots of meetings so I decided to get all Power Suit-y. My Power Suit is black, with a jacket and a sort of sleeveless dress thing underneath. Wearing the Power Suit makes me feel like giving orders and making decisions and crossing things off the to-do list. In other words, wearing the Power Suit makes me feel like a cliché. This cliché feeling was further en-

hanced by the fact that yesterday morning I called home
to ask LT to pick up my dry cleaning. All I lacked yesterday, in the cliché department, was a personal assistant to
follow me around with a clipboard and say, "Yes, Ms.
Smartypants" a lot, and bring me tea, and then at some
point I would, in a completely unethical, immoral, and
illegal fashion, turn the personal assistant into my personal fuckpuppet, and give the personal assistant the best
sex of the personal assistant's young and inexperienced
life, and then I would fire the personal assistant when I
got bored. The personal assistant would cry all alone in
the personal assistant's studio apartment, and from then
on the personal assistant would have an ever-more-
intense craving and weakness for Power Suit–wearing
ambitious and determined brunettes, and would be
henceforth unable to form any meaningful relationships
with anyone who did not fit into this category. Cliché
fantasies like these are all side effects of the Power Suit,
which makes me think that perhaps I shouldn't wear the
Power Suit too often.

Also, the Power Suit resulted in a lot more attention
from men than is customary. I was cartoon-wolf-whistled
at from a pickup truck while I waited for the bus, and all
during the workday it seemed like random guys from the
building made small talk with me in the elevator, held the
door open, and so on. Or maybe this is how all grown-up
women who routinely wear Power Suits are treated, and I
have just been missing out on the chivalry because of my
normal business attire, which falls mostly into the following categories:

a. Slightly Gothic First-Grader;
b. I-Still-Am-Cool-Goddammit-Even-Though-I'm-Thirty Thrift Store Finds;
c. Some Sort of Black Garment from the Laundry Pile; or everyone's winter favorite,
d. Long Skirt, Big Sweater, and Tough-Girl Boots

There is some meeting going on about changes in the pension plan at work. We all received an insanely upbeat e-mail about how this investment company is going to come talk to us about all the new, fresh, fun, and funky mutual funds that are available for us to invest in. I was bored so I e-mailed around a fake prospectus that I made up lampooning this crap, and it included such fake mutual funds as:

• The Militia Index (a diversified portfolio of Bibles, guns, bottled water, and gold)
• ColombiaCartelCorp (with the Dow in the toilet, there's never been a better time to invest in cocaine)
• GlobalCollective's Blood of the Proletariat Fund (fantastic growth opportunity, just get out before the revolution comes!)

And so forth. No matter how busy I get at work, there is always time for making fun of stuff.

TINY MYSTERIES OF LIFE

1. A very weird subject line for spam: Watch Me Film Myself Masturbating. Whoa. That's pretty removed from the subject/object consciousness. Can't I just watch you masturbating? I have to watch "the making of" you masturbating? Maybe this particular cam-girl is a staunch foe of reductionist realism, and is interested in a transcendentalist vision of her masturbating that moves toward an idealization of forms. Maybe.

2. The way that pairs of shoelaces, lightbulbs in adjacent rooms, and rolls of toilet paper in bathrooms one and two all break/burn out/get used up within days, sometimes hours, of each other.

3. The (short, stunted, mushroom-clammy, and pale, smelled a bit like a boiled vegetable) guy who sat next to me on the train and crossed himself before opening a textbook about how to program in FORTRAN. (Tiny mystery **3a:** Why are you learning how to program in FORTRAN?)

Yesterday LT and I had an appointment in Evanston (I took the bus from work, he met me there with the car). On the way back we were driving down Ridge and I saw someone we went to school with, and she's trying to drive alongside us and get a better look at me too, so I say to LT, "Hey, that's Susan _____." Only instead of saying the last name of Susan, who at college was a sort of hippie-ish Park Ranger–type girl, who loved camping and biology and hockey, and who dealt LSD for a while, I said the last name of a campus professor, also named Susan, who was a to-the-right-of-Ashcroft born-again Christian political science professor. (I know. It was not a felicitous combination.) So LT was initially kind of confused with my directions to pull over and converse with said Susan. But we did, and chatted and exchanged numbers, and she even lives near our neighborhood as it turns out.

After that injection of college nostalgia we were exhausted, and hungry, and my memory was totally failing me as to whether we had any food in the house. I kept trying to mentally picture the contents of the refrigerator and the cupboards and was not coming up with anything. In fact, whenever I tried to picture what was in the refrigerator, my brain returned an image of a Frisbee with some spinach leaves and sun-dried tomatoes artfully arranged on top of it. Artful as it may be, it doesn't make for a very satisfying dinner experience, so we stopped at Ethiopian Diamond for a vegetarian combo. I can recommend the yatakilt wat without reservation.

Tonight I am having a very quick after-work drink with a friend and then I am kind of floating around the city. Of course, I could be sensible and go home afterward, and take vitamins and drink pure fresh mountain spring water and go to sleep at a reasonable hour. But then I wouldn't be living up to my tough Power Suit image. (By the way, if that report isn't on my desk by the end of the day . . .)

← *July 26*

Today I leaned over the sink and spat toothpaste right on my arm. Right on the sleeve of my shirt. So I had to change, right before leaving the house. Charming.

I don't know why I'm surprised anymore when I do boneheaded things. I am the person who knocked down part of my parents' garage when I was trying to park. (I don't drive anymore.) I've knocked down construction barriers and then driven over them. Once, when I still smoked (and when I still drove), I lit a cigarette with the car's cigarette lighter, waved the cigarette lighter in the air briefly, and then threw it out the window as if it were a match. That one was fun to explain to my parents.

Other smoking-related accidents: I remember trying to get an ashtray off a very high shelf in the campus café, just getting the edge of it with my fingers, and consequently dumping the entire ashtray on my head.

I went home, showered, and went back to bed.

Not as bad as my friend Eric, though, who has a story about dropping his contact lens into a full ashtray. Not very hygienic.

I once put both contact lenses into the same eye. Unfortunately, I did not end up with X-ray vision.

Some sort of air show is happening today. As we speak, jet fighters are zooming over my building, making all sorts of non-office-type noises, and every once in a while I'll glance up to see a plane spinning wildly or plunging straight down over the lake or something like that.

I hope those stunt pilots aren't as absentminded as I sometimes am.

⸺ July 28

I happened to step into the mini-mailroom collection point on my office floor, to post my electric bill, just as the young and rather strapping Mailroom Boy was emptying the bins. It was one of those awkward step-around-you encounters, where I was entering and he was leaving, and he said "I'll take that," meaning he would stick my envelope with his other recently collected mail. "Ulp, ah sure, okay," I said, like the biggest dork around, and handed it to him, and then on the way out I even more awkwardly banged into the doorway, because I am kind of clumsy sometimes. The elbow banging made a loud clunking noise, but it did not hurt.

"Oh man, are you okay?" asks Mailroom Boy.

"Yeah," I say, still trying to make my awkward escape from the room. "Good thing I have a titanium elbow, ha ha!"

"Really? How did that happen?"

I look at him and see that he totally believes me, and because there is some *Crucial synapse problem* in my brain that prevents me from occasionally lying to strangers, I spin a brief yarn about a long-ago bike accident that shattered my elbow, and he is all surfer dude, "That sucks!" and then we make some jokes about setting off metal detectors, and then I flee. And spend the next few hours kicking myself. The Girl Who Cried Titanium Elbow.

←July 29

Last night I went out for Italian food with my sister-in-law, to a lovely little restaurant on Armitage, and because I am clumsy I dropped a mushroom piece on my skirt, and then later I splashed a tiny bit of wine on myself (these were not alcohol-related accidents, I swear, I just talk with my hands too much), and in the process of a self-deprecating description of my follies and pointing out the stains I said, "I'm a full meal from the waist down" (meaning entree plus beverage). It sounded a lot naughtier than I meant it to be.

⟵ *August 1*

BRAND-NEW DRINKING GAMES

1. Smashy-Smashy Smash Everything in the Goddamned Place

2. Eavesdrop and Then Make Fun of Other People's Stupid Conversations

3. No Beer Bottle Labels Allowed (Peelapalooza)

4. Arm Wrestling with Strangers

5. Embarrassing Personal Revelations (aka Time-Release Regret Capsule)

6. Throw a Punch at Your Best Friend

7. Persistence of Memory (aka 1–800–GET–BAIL)

⟵ *August 2*

I am quite bored right now. Our database, which contains manuscripts and articles (in short, my reason for being here), is broken, and as the day drags on it doesn't look like the computer nerds are going to be successful in fixing it anytime soon. I was passing the time by playing this little online Shockwave video game called Smite Thee, in which you, as deity, bless the believers who are carrying offerings and strike down the unbelievers who are destroying your temple, but of course I did not read the directions until later and played the game several times just smiting everyone indiscriminately. I am a capricious god.

Last night there was a very weird smell in our living room. It smelled like a beauty parlor, like that permanent wave solution. LT and I sniffed everywhere, went down to the basement to check for gas leaks, confirmed that it wasn't coming from outside, confirmed that it was confined to the living room, and generally wandered around puzzled. I imagined I was getting dizzy but I think that was mostly from breathing deeply as I tried to smell the smell. We turned off the lights in the living room and strangely, that seemed to help, although it definitely wasn't an electrical type of smell but, as previously stated, a beauty salon type of smell. Now I'm worried that (1) there's some sort of toxic substance in the apartment and The Cat's little cat lungs are becoming damaged or (2) it really was electrical and our apartment is burning down as we speak.

Don't say it don't say it don't say it! Yes, my hyperbolic neuroses are very amusing and everything, but remember this is Crazy Obsessive-Compulsive Me. I really have had this low-level anxiety about these things all day and it's driving me nuts. I don't know of any way to check on the safety and integrity of my house and cat other than going home and checking on them, which I cannot do because I am at work, and which I also cannot do because that's just too crazy. As in, leaving the realm of the Amusing Crazy and crossing over into Pathetic and Sad and in Need of Medication Crazy.

Okay, I'm going to work on calm.

━━━ *August 4*

LIES I HAVE TOLD SPONTANEOUSLY THAT OTHER PEOPLE BELIEVED

1. I told a really stupid girl in college that my plans for the summer involved working on a Jamaican sugarcane plantation.

2. I told a different really stupid girl in college that I had killed someone once. "It was sort of an accident," I said. "I don't like to talk about it."

3. I told a guy at a bar that I was once hospitalized because I stuck an entire ballpoint pen up my nose and it punctured a sinus.

4. I told my seventh-grade gym teacher that I could not play soccer that day because it was a religious holiday for my family, and that we were Rosicrucians. He wasn't quite sure so he let me go to the library for that period, but he did call my mom that night. Damn.

━━━ *August 5*

I was at the drugstore the other day. You know, a lot of my sentences start like that. When am I ever not at the freaking drugstore? Apparently I spend my life buying toiletries. Anyway, I was extremely tempted to buy *Cosmopolitan* magazine, which I honestly hate but with which I have a sort of sick fascination. The reason I was so tempted was that this issue had a corner cut advertising it as the "Bad Girl" issue. Be still my heart! What a great evening that would be for a deeply sarcastic feminist freak like myself . . . sit back, crack open a beer, and peruse the "Bad Girl" issue. Ah bliss.

Exit (a bar/nightclub) used to have (and maybe still does) a pinball machine that had the theme of "Bad Girls." It said BAD GIRLS! in huge red slasher-movie-font letters, and an illustration of two women in lingerie and high heels lounging on the hood of a sports car. I used to wonder: now what makes these girls "bad"? They are underdressed, perhaps, maybe even skanky, but "bad" seems like an awfully pejorative judgment to make. Instead of labeling them "bad," maybe we could get to know them. Lend them a sweater and some pants, share part of our lunch. Let them into our jump rope circle at recess. Show them that there is more to life than posing on the hood of a car in lingerie.

◄━ August 8

Yesterday I was up in Andersonville and I saw Screaming Man. It was quite a shock, for I always thought Screaming Man was a strictly downtown citizen. For those of you who are not familiar, Screaming Man is a middle-aged, very tall, bearded black guy who wears a whole lot of scarves and rags and fabric strips tied kerchief-style around his head.

And yes, he screams, wordlessly and at semiregular intervals. I recognized him immediately as I rounded the corner of Berwyn and Clark, and my first thought was to ask, "Hey Screaming Man! What the heck are you doing this far north?" But I didn't.

◄— *August 11*

Day six of being a Phlegm Machine, more of a low-grade annoyance than a full-blown pestilence, which has afforded me the opportunity to enter the wonderful world of over-the-counter drug experimentation. I feel like I have tried every cold medicine under the sun at this point. None is completely satisfactory, but all have interesting side effects.

There's Tylenol Cold, which makes my eyeballs twitch and gives me the feeling that something is sneaking up at the edge of my peripheral vision. There's Nyquil, which sends me to some Land of Unconsciousness that is not quite sleep and makes me dream that my hands are very large. There's Comtrex Severe Congestion capsules, which work a bit too well, and drain my head so completely that I can feel my dry brain rattling around like a seed in the gourd of my skull. I've tried Robitussin, too, with the thought that if I can't block the production of phlegm perhaps I can at least change its consistency, but since I took the recommended dose and not the whole bottle, it really just did exactly what it was purported to do. (Note: what is with kids these days? Someone please get them some proper drugs.)

My unusual-side-effect profile is not limited to over-the-counter drugs: prescription drugs too have caused me to act strangely. (Oh, Mimi, but how would we know the difference? you cry. Ha ha. Oh, it is to laugh.) My very brief experience with psychiatric medication proves a useful case in point: I once tried an old-skool antidepressant that made me have extremely vivid yet prosaic dreams, to the point where I couldn't distinguish what had really happened and what hadn't and would go into detail with baffled friends about conversations we never had and trips to the mall that did not occur. It also made food taste like cardboard representations of food. But I really think the most interesting unanticipated side effect was that it made me horny beyond belief, and capable of deriving shivering, eyelid-fluttering sensual enjoyment from the most minor tactile sensations. I know what you're thinking: and you discontinued this medication exactly why? But seriously folks, it's no way to live, when you can go into a trance simply by rubbing your own cashmere-sweatered arm, when scratching your own neck will cause little fast-motion flowers to bloom in the brain, and when you have to stop taking the bus because the rumbling idle of the motor is just too much. It's hard to get anything done that way. Not to mention the fact that although your significant other will think that it's all very charming and erotic that you're ready to pay the check with just a bit of ear-licking, he or she will still be waiting for the meal to be served, if you get my drift, and I think you do. So long story short, no more psychiatric medication for me, and these days I just deal, sometimes well, sometimes badly, with whatever my brain decides to dish out.

On Milwaukee Avenue there is a very baffling store. It is called Wigs and Plus. As if "plus" were a noun all to itself. Also, the redundancy. That store wants to be called Wigs Plus Plus. Doubleplus wigthink ungood!

It is alarming (if you are like me and are easily alarmed) that one can just walk in off the street and buy a wig. And then wear a wig. Just like it is no big deal. There should be a waiting period for wig wearing like there is for gun buying.

I think I am having an attack of nerves. I feel tired, trembly, and weird. The parsimonious explanation for my trembly weirdness and inappropriate giggling and need to sit all contorted and strange would be not enough sleep and too much jittersauce last night. (That is an old slang term for liquor, and I provide this parenthetical explanation in case you did not know that, and your imagination was postulating that I have switched vices, from beer to amphetamine-laced applesauce. Although, right about now, the idea of amphetamine-laced applesauce sounds kind of attractive. I'll bring the trucker speed if you bring the Mott's.)

Wow. I am completely amazed at my mental hyperlinks, but I really do have a story to tell about drugs and applesauce. My college was too small to have its own health service, but it had contracted with a couple of doctors in town to treat us crazy mixed-up kids for free. There was this one old doctor on Main Street who was widely known around campus for handing out all kinds of pills. He was very generous with the controlled narcotics, often giving away free samples even if you didn't ask or hint or anything. Because of this he was very popular. At the time I was getting these incredibly painful cluster headaches, and one day I just couldn't take it anymore so I went to see him. And he gave me samples of Xanax, which is not even appropriate for headaches, and suggested that I take one before leaving his office. I dutifully did so, partly because hey why not get a little loopy, I've got no more classes today, and partly because he *is* a doctor, even if a sketchy one, and my head hurt so bad I was willing to try anything. I swallowed the Xanax and it hit me hard on the walk back to campus, floating over the lawn with an angelic faraway grin on my face, and it was dinnertime so I showed up at the cafeteria. My friends were well versed in the ways of Substances so they immediately knew something was up, but I was too stoned to try and explain it to them, and too stoned to even think about chewing food, so I got a bowl of applesauce and sat back down. I was swirling the applesauce around and watching it drip off the spoon and being very quiet, and everyone kind of forgot about me, until I started scraping the spoon back and forth on the bowl in a rhythmic fashion and suddenly interrupted the whole table's conversation to say, "Guess what song I'm playing in my applesauce!" That became a sort of drug-taking catchphrase at school, and it was very embarrassing and I never did live it down, and I cannot believe that I have told this story here.

This entry was written in two parts, which is unusual for me (because this diary is nothing if not slapdash). The writing of it was split by an Emergency Nap. I don't know if you have the same violent mood-swing issues that I do, but I was bustling around the house feeling very useful and good, and then I was sitting here computering for a while, and suddenly it was like a giant butterfly net scooped me up and threw me into an old mayonnaise jar, and didn't poke any holes in the top of the jar, and everything started to look cheap and two-dimensional and relentlessly ugly and pointless, and I could feel my shoulders creeping up around my ears and my brow starting to furrow, and thus I literally had to drop everything and with a firm sense of purpose did not pass Go, did not collect any warm human feelings, but went straight to the bedroom and crawled under the blankets. Ninety minutes later I was a much nicer person.

← August 18

It must be a huge allergy day here in Chicago, the mold or pollen count way up, because my eyes are itching like crazy. And I'm wearing mascara. These two things combined are unfortunate, since I keep forgetting I'm wearing mascara (it's not an everyday thing for me) and rubbing my eye in that little-kid-sleepy or allergic-adult way, and coming away with my fingertips all black.

I thought of a use for the Room with No Purpose. LT and I have a three-bedroom place. One bedroom is for sleeping, one bedroom is LT's office, where he does all the freelance computer programming, and one is just empty. I have been rather adamant about leaving it empty until we come up for an actual use for it, because I don't want to just start treating it as a giant closet by default, because then it becomes the Room We Need to Store Crap In. Some ideas we have considered thus far have been Tiki Room, Disco Room, Library, and filling it with row upon row of identical garden gnomes (think ancient China's terracotta soldiers) and referring to them as "my minions." But now I think I want it to be a Situation Room. You know, like in the Pentagon. We could get a huge conference table and a bunch of pull-down maps. The next time The Cat threatens to deploy one of her suicide bombing missions, LT and I could meet in the Situation Room and discuss how best to thwart her evil plan.

← August 19

Last night I went with a group of people to this fancy schmancy "pub" that had lots of esoteric and imported beers. I am somewhat clueless when it comes to beer this fancy, so I let someone else order for me, and when he brought the beer back to the table he told me its name was "Alpha King." Only I am going deaf and thought he said "Elfin King." So this amused me, and throughout that entire round of drinks I would occasionally break away from the conversation and say things like, "He's the King of the Elves!" or "All hail the tiny King!" and "I wonder if they brewed this in a hollow tree?" And so on. After about an hour someone asked me what the fuck I was talking about and the true name of the beer was revealed.

What I found so disturbing was that my friends took my

psychotic exclamations in stride and waited *so long* to question me. What does that say about me? Do I normally say all sorts of bizarre things? I didn't think so before, but now I'm not so sure.

← *August 21*

Sometimes you (yes, even you!) need a reminder not to take yourself quite so seriously. One of the methods I use to remember not to take myself so seriously is an incident from college. I had dropped a large amount of acid with friends, but at this particular moment I was in Introspective Mode, because I had decided I had Things to Figure Out. Anyway, there was an ice storm this night, and at the time I was in the downstairs window seat in our big old house enjoying the swirling snowstorm, and enjoying the layered effect of the cross-hatched chickenwire safety glass, the ice ferning on the window, and of course the patterns and colors from my brain. I noticed this pattern roaming around out there in the snowflakes, and I decided with typical drug-addled pretentiousness that this pattern was going to resolve into a hallucination that would Tell Me Something. So I waited and watched, and the pattern swirled and bulged and rippled and eventually resolved itself into Astro, the dog from *The Jetsons.*

Hee hee hee! So while I don't discount the validity of anyone else's Moment of Clarity, drug-induced or otherwise, make sure you take a second to reflect and ascertain that you are not simply being a pretentious dork. I consider that particular hallucination a sort of warning signal from my brain that things were getting a little too pompous and serious up there.

◄─── *August 22*

Remember that part in the movie *Big Night* when the chef, talking about some dish he had in Italy, screams, "It is so good you will want to *kill* yourself! One bite and you will *not want to live*!"

It's been a while since I had food that good. The now-sadly-closed Buona Fortuna, which used to be on Milwaukee Avenue, had a gnocchi with Gorgonzola cream sauce that didn't exactly make me want to kill myself, but I would have been willing to maim myself a little. And then today I had a brownie from an overpriced yuppie sandwich shop. This brownie is $2.50, which is rather pricey for a brownie. (Especially for a brownie without, you know, mind-altering properties.) But oh man. It was so good I closed the office door while I ate it, to avoid any interruptions. I tried to carefully balance the amount of tea I had left with the dwindling brownie so the mix would come out just right. It was fudgy and chocolaty and so good kings and princes would fall to their knees and beg me for a taste. But no. "Get your own," I would say.

◄─── *August 23*

Yawn. I'm weary from the strain of (a) working after four days off, (b) once again being forced to wear real pants

after spending so much of those four days off in my pajamas (it's not fair, the tyranny of enforced real-pants-
wearing in the business world. I look quite fetching in my
pajamas), and (c) dealing with some insane micromanage-
ment and tomfoolery in the office. Today I showed another
adult person, who makes much more money than I do and
is supposedly in a position of authority, how to make fold-
ers on her hard drive. She was fussing about all the memos
and e-mails and documents she had to track, and I happened to mention that I had all of mine in one convenient
folder, and she asked, "Well, how do you get a folder?"
Hmmm. I mean, I'm not Little Miss Microsoft or anything,
but there's a pull-down menu for *New. Folder.* And that
(wow!) would be how you get a new folder (amazing!).

◄—— *August 24*

Marketers must think that if you are vegetarian you are
also a kook. That's the explanation I have for the fact that
I regularly receive an invitation to join this weird book club
of "New Age" volumes, all about how the angels are going
to help you start your own business and crap like that. I always look at the catalog, though, just to get a handle on
what odd things are out there, and this time I found a book
called *Zen Sex*, billed as being written by the same man who
wrote *Zen Guitar*. The problems are threefold: (1) there is a
book called *Zen Sex*, (2) there is a book called *Zen Guitar*,
and (3) the man who wrote *Zen Guitar* is qualified to write
Zen Sex. Why do I imagine a really creepy sandal-wearing
guy who invites you up to his room to play "Moondance"

for you on his acoustic? And when are the world's Buddhists going to get sick of all this crap and start laying the smackdown on people?

← August 25

Overheard conversation between two tough-looking gangsta guys (Latin Kings? There was lots of black and gold clothing involved):

King One: ". . . and then this motherfucker tells me he's moving to Nova Scotia."
King Two: "Damn."
King One: "Nova fucking *Scotia*! I'm telling you!"

← August 26

My I Am a Superhuman Uberfrau and I Don't Need to Sleep phase has ended, I think, for the time being. Night after night of too little slow-wave sleep came smashing down on me like a stack of plates in the arms of a drunken waiter, who will be fired as soon as he gets to the end of his shift, and he'll go home and smoke a joint and think about how it's not fair, his whole life is such a fucking mess, and why should he have to work anyway, he's an *artist* and he can't be held to the bullshit societal standards of the workaday world, and then at 3 A.M. he'll put on his old Replacements records and sing along loudly until the neighbors pound on the walls.

The consequences of the Smashing Plate Stack of Not Enough Quality Sleep are that I am really spacey and sleepy and strange, and in order not to doze off on the train this morning (I don't like sleeping on the El, even in the safe and commuter-friendly mornings, because you never know when a pickpocket or a public masturbator will strike), I had to jiggle my leg and chew the inside of my cheek and tap out Vivaldi concertos with my fingers, which, hey guess what! makes me look like one of those colorful subway crazies I always talk about! What goes around comes around, Mimi Smartypants!

HERE COMES THE BORING PART ABOUT MY MUSIC LESSONS

I went to my violin lesson and Paul gave me a huge amount of practice material and homework (luckily I won't have another lesson for two weeks). We spent some time on third-position intonation, and discovered I have pinky-finger issues, and have to seriously contort and stretch and twist my hand/arm/elbow/wrist in order to throw the finger out far enough. All of a sudden Paul stopped talking and took my violin, holding it up and staring at it for a long time. "Try mine," he said, and handed me his instrument. I played the same passage and my mouth fell open. *It was easy.* No ridiculous stretch, no contortion that breaks the whole flow of the piece, no sketchy intonation. "Your fingerboard is too long," he said. "Your whole violin is built on a slightly larger scale than mine." We got out a measuring tape and sure enough, my fingerboard was a tiny bit larger than his, and little differences mean a lot when you are talking about something with the need for precise delicate adjustments like a violin. And remember, I have little puny paws and he has big huge mitts, so the difference was even more pronounced.

My question is: *how did this happen?* Who steered me wrong? I bought my instrument right before I started high school, and of course I went to the snooty downtown violin store and tried many different instruments (before eventually buying mine someplace less snooty), and I don't remember having this pinky-finger intonation problem back then. So there are two possibilities: (1) my violin has always been slightly too large for me, and my teacher at the time as well as the instrument consultant who helped me buy it were just idiots and didn't notice; or (2) I am shrinking.

What to do about this bizarre musical problem:

1. Deal with it. Find fingering workarounds (although you do have to use your pinky finger at some point, no matter what). Tune slightly sharp and avoid open strings as much as possible.

2. Science. Have an engineer develop a large bendy cyberhand to replace mine. Fly to Mexico or Sweden and have some sort of experimental hand-stretching surgery.

3. Buy a new, correctly sized, violin. (Oh sure. Let me just go get that extra eight grand I keep in the sock drawer.) (Then again, there's always crime: who wants to help me go knock over a liquor store or three? It's for a good cause.)

4. When Paul's not looking, switch my instrument with his.

TWO MINOR TOTAL-STRANGER BUS ENCOUNTERS

1. I saw a guy wearing three baseball caps all at the same time, stacked one on top of the other.

2. A teenage boy (with the requisite big pants and bad posture) caught my eye and said, "Is that a violin?" When I said yes, he affected extreme casual disinterest and asked, "What school do you go to?" while simultaneously blushing a bit. It was so damn cute and yet I am way too elderly to still get chatted up by high school boys on the city bus. I blame the ponytail.

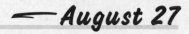

August 27

TEN PIÑATAS OF NOTE: RESERVE NOW FOR YOUR NEXT BIRTHDAY PARTY

1. Drug Mule Piñata (worried-looking papier-mâché dude: inside are condoms full of heroin)

2. Dead Animal Piñata

3. Piñata Full of Leftover Hair Clippings from the Barbershop (drifting down, sticking to the sweaty children)

4. Piñata Full of Pudding

5. Dirty Piñata (full of radioactive material)

6. Piñata Full of Broken Glass and Nails (the Terrorist Special)

7. Piñata Full of Porn

8. Piñata Full of Ball Bearings

9. Piñata Full of Useful Toiletries (tampons, unbreakable combs, acne medicine)

10. Zen Piñata (full of nothing)

◂— *August 30*

AS THOUGH OF HEMLOCK I HAD DRUNK

Today I am afflicted with dizzy spells, and my spine feels like glass, and I hurt in all the bendy places. Plus I have a touch of maudlin Frowny Mouth Syndrome. Last night I proved my fuckwittedness once again by leaving some important paperwork in a cab. I remember what kind of cab but not, of course, the number, and I called immediately when I got home and again just now, and filled out their little online lost and found form in great detail, but apparently my bag containing important paperwork (and, less importantly, a Talking Heads CD and an ugly skirt I had planned to return) has not been turned in yet. If I don't hear anything by the end of the day tomorrow I will have to start the process of replacing and recreating the important paperwork, and my spine feels even glassier and my mouth more frowny as I think about that. There is nothing worse than suffering caused through one's own stupidity; I think that just about everyone would rather be a victim than an idiot. If only a giant pterodactyl from the distant past had swooped down and stolen my important paperwork. If only I had been surrounded by murderous ninjas and had to hurl my important paperwork at them in order to escape. But no, I just left it in a taxicab (sober, even!). Sigh.

(I am making too much of this, I know, but I am feeling dramatic. Leave me alone.)

⟵ *September 2*

Today I had to go to the doctor for a physical.

VARIOUS MEDICAL THOUGHTS

- Those paper gowns are horrible. And baffling. I turned the stupid thing this way and that, and accidentally ended up ripping it some in my efforts to unfold it. So I had a punk rock paper gown. I would rather just sit there naked, honestly, than feel like a total idiot draped in a large piece of crackly paper.

- They left me in the exam room too long by myself, so I got bored and stole some tongue depressors. I also took a pamphlet about bacterial vaginosis because the cover made me laugh: it spoke of "the #1 Vaginal Infection." It was a photo finish at the Vaginal Infection World Championships! Bacterial vaginosis beat out candidiasis by a narrow margin! On the exam room wall was a large poster about the spine that made me feel even more pale and sickly. I don't like vertebrae. I couldn't look at it.

- I found out that I have been consistently overestimating my weight, probably for years. (I don't own a scale, so the doctor is the only time I ever find out the truth.) I secretly want to be big and tough.

- After the physical they wanted blood from me. I have barely any veins to speak of (I would make a lousy heroin addict), and the lab technician had to use yards of rubber tubing and slap my arm for about an hour, and even then she still had to stab me three times in each arm. They filled up two large tubes and now I feel all deflated, like a sad beach toy. So I called in a pint low and took the rest of the day off.

- There was also a request made for some of my pee, and I didn't really have to go so I had kind of a scanty little specimen cup. Which triggered an immediate flash of guilt in my brain. Which in turn made me laugh at myself for being such a Type A overachiever who feels guilty at not being able to produce a whole lot of urine on demand.

◄— *September 5*

Lipstick and I have a difficult relationship. Sometimes I am friends with lipstick all day and then suddenly at the end of the night I feel like lipstick just has to go, *now*, and I start compulsively rubbing at my lips like a long-term speed freak who feels the crawly bugs under her skin. Last night I am standing at the bar, patiently waiting my turn, and a very drunk man in a leather jacket hands me an empty shot glass and slurs, "Why don't you get some lipstick on that." Then he leans in all conspiratorial drunk and says, "Or you could put lipstick somewhere else, know what I mean?" "No. I don't," I say, and give him Icy Blank Stare #36 (I have forty-two Icy Blank Stares in total). Although I prefer to solve most of my problems with violence, I think that went pretty well. Besides, if I keep busting fingers by punching people all the time, I will have arthritis in ten years, minimum. Score one for maturity.

⟵ *September 6*

Okay, it's confession time. I have always had a tiny crush on Al Gore. Once, on business, I stayed in the same hotel at the same time as Al Gore, and I got vaguely excited by the thought that somewhere above or below me Al Gore was possibly showering or taking off his pants. So of course, even though it makes me into a bit of a stalker (or at least a big weirdo), when Al Gore came through Chicago on a bookstore tour I had to be there.

IN WHICH I ATTEND AL GORE'S
BOOK-SIGNING APPEARANCE

Let my love open the Gore
Let my love open *the Gore*
Let my love open the Gore
the Al Gore

1, 2, 3, 4 Get your former vice prez on the floor
Gotta get up to get down

Look over there, it's MC Al Gore
He's hard to catch like the albacore
He's hard to destroy like uranium ore

A to the L to the G-O-R-E
Speaking his rhymes to the petite bourgeoisie

Okay, so I can't rap.

SOME SNIPPETS FROM THE ALGOREXTRAVAGANZA

- There were no refreshments. No cake shaped like Al Gore's head. No Goresicles. No Goreos.
- There was, however, an incredible lack of organization. There were two groups of people to see Al Gore; my sister and I were in the first, smaller (two hundred or so people) group. The organizers, and I use that term loosely, just opened the floodgates to the venue (which, somewhat strangely, was the Swedish-American Museum on Clark Street). They checked to make sure you had a blue ticket and a book, but that was about it. Then everyone sort of crowded around the front of the museum, jockeying for position like at a rock show, while a lady with a very shrill voice explained the "event guidelines" to us *three times*, despite the fact that we had all received them in a handout moments ago. It was annoying, but I suffered through it, because I was ready to Get My Gore On.
- Eventually Al and Tipper showed up to make their "remarks." Al looked fine in the standard political navy suit and reddish tie. He had really pink cheeks, probably from all the Scotch he was drinking backstage. (Just kidding! Oh, let's all get sued for libel! Oh goody, do let's! That will be ever so much fun!)

(Where did that *Little Women* diction come from? I think I have a fever.)

- Al's remarks were kind of ranty. Not crazy-ranty, but sort of all over the place about the changes (good and bad) in the historical American family. The man sure likes his statistics. Tipper's remarks were much less interesting and more subdued, but maybe she gets tired having to stand there and fake like she is adoringly listening to Al all the time.

- I made a llama puppet (it's a long story) and I wanted the llama to be able to see Al Gore. I stuck my arm up in the air so the puppet could look out over the crowd, and I learned that the Secret Service *really* do not like it when you show a puppet to someone they are protecting. No tackling ensued, but two of the guys moved over to get a better view of me and stayed like that for the rest of the remarks. My sister and I developed a fondness for the Secret Service and decided that we want to get some old phone cord and make fake curly ear wire things for ourselves like the ones they have. It looks really cool.

- I know I sound like a stalker when I say this, but Al Gore was totally looking at me several times. Or maybe he was just freaked out by the llama, too.

- Then we got in line to have our books signed. It moved slowly. We were in line near these middle-aged Total Stress Kittens, women with too much makeup who kept whining about "personal space" and the temperature in the room. I can't stand it when people feel the need to make loud remarks like that. If you are truly freaked out by crowds, then leave. If you are just cranky and a big Complainer Head, keep your mouth shut where others can hear you because we cannot do anything about it. At one point one of them says, "And this woman is totally blocking me in," so I turn to her and say in a steely monotone, "Would that be *me* you are discussing? Am I blocking you in or otherwise causing you trauma?" She says, "Oh, no, no" and gestures to some other total stranger, but I think I made my point.

- Here is simultaneously the best and worst part. I get up to the book-signing table, and Al Gore is sitting down behind the table so really there is no way to de-pants him without diving onto the floor and causing a major scene, and you can't really de-pants someone when they are in a seated position anyway. I am not too disappointed because it is not like I live in a no-pants Al Gore fantasy world. Really. Al Gore signs my book, shakes my hand, and says "Thank you for coming" or one of his stock phrases. Then he squints at me and says, "What is that?"

"That" is this button on my coat. My sister makes buttons. She makes them collage-style, just cutting out random images and text and pressing them into a button. I have one that features a bored-looking medieval woman with a book on her head, chin resting on her fist, and the found text says BOY AM I IMPRESSED.

"That's funny," says Al Gore. And chuckles. Gore-riffically.

But oh no, I think as I walk away. I hope that Al Gore does not think my button, which I totally forgot about and which has just been riding around on my coat for a month, is some sort of cynical disaffected commentary on the Al Gore Scene. It is my cynical disaffected commentary on the world in general, plus I just really like the image, but *it has nothing to do with you Al Gore*. I am currently drafting a letter to this effect.

◄━━ *September 9*

A SHORT COLLECTION OF SOME OF THE MOST BACKHANDED COMPLIMENTS I HAVE EVER RECEIVED

1. "I find it comforting that someone as fucked in the head as you has made such a success of her life."

2. "Your breasts are plenty large enough for my purposes."

3. "I could never wear something like that, but you are able to pull it off somehow."

4. [After I'd expressed various strong opinions and come to the passionate defense of my department during a business meeting] "We appreciate your input and, uh, vigor."

5. "Mimi, you have a very unusual sense of humor. Sometimes it takes effort to understand you."

◄━━ *September 10*

Lost weekend. Not in the usual sense that I got all bedrunken and I don't quite remember anything past our

conversation about ballpoint pens. Nor in the *X-Files* sense
that I was abducted by the gray people with the big heads
and subjected to anal probing, although really, that might
have been preferable compared to the other bodily un-
pleasantness I suffered this weekend, which included a
nonstop cough; painful, swollen throat; gallons of some
substance (maybe ectoplasm? Follow up with that alien
theory) suffusing my sinuses and ears; and an ungovern-
able exhaustion that made it seem like a lot of trouble to
move my arms and legs or even my eyeballs. (At one point
LT asked, "Are you okay?" because I wasn't responding to
anything he said, and I could only sort of flop my hand at
him in what I hoped was a reassuring gesture.) Saturday I
did literally nothing but sleep and get up every four to six
hours to swallow cough syrup. LT, because he is a propo-
nent of the healthy Smartypants and because he is just
generally a compassionate guy, went out to our sketchy
drugstore for me at eight o'clock in the morning, stood in
line at the register behind all our neighborhood's alco-
holics, with their shaking hands and their six-packs of Nat-
ural Light (goes down smooth and easy!) and bottles of
Grand Marnier (almost like orange juice!), and returned
home with a wide array of cough medicine for me to
choose from, plus the latest issue of *Cosmopolitan*.

TIME OUT FOR PRESCRIPTIVE LITERATURE RANT, WHICH YOU HAVE HEARD BEFORE BUT I CAN'T HELP MYSELF

Cosmo. Wow. Now listen, I *know* that fashion magazines
are up to no good. But still, I see them so seldom that when
I actually take a look I am flabbergasted all over again. It is

all about the high heels and the landing-a-man plan, and the "career advice" seems directed to women who work as entry-level eye candy in fields where being seen in this season's Prada is more important than being seen making decisions and handling yourself like an adult. (Seriously, if you need to be told not to cry at work, and not to sleep with your boss, maybe you are not ready for a real job.) Here is the bit that got to me, though: The Seven Sex Tricks You Must Know suggested that you "keep him guessing" and "mix things up." How to put this into practice? When he starts to go down on you, *stop the action and go down on him instead*. Really. It really said that. Besides the ever-present mixed messages (are women supposed to be insatiable sex kittens or submissive man pleasers?), *can we afford to be passing up oral sex action?* If we pass up oral sex action, in the manner that *Cosmo* so cavalierly suggests, the terrorists win. Sisters. Do it for America.

Anyway, I spent the weekend, as I said before, completely wacked out on cough syrup, to the point where *Cosmo*'s "Bedside Astrologer" started to make sense to me. ("Why yes," I thought. "As a Capricorn, I indeed am 'all business in the bedroom,' and totally adept at turning my partner into 'passion putty'!") (What *is* it with *Cosmo* and alliteration?)

At least I had the good sense to get sick on an autumn Sunday, when football (hooray!) is on television all day. I think I fell asleep on the couch during the game and dreamed that the Colts made a field goal, and that the Jets beat them 41–3 instead of 41–0. I don't mind the Jets winning at all, a jet plane is way cooler than a baby horse, but they do make me angry in one respect: the old quarterback, now sadly sidelined, was Vinny Testaverde,* which is a totally kick-ass name and appropriately working class for what is essentially a New Jersey team. The new, winninger quarterback is named Chad Pennington, and don't you just want to punch that name in the mouth? That is a name that John Hughes would make up for the bastard who would not take Molly Ringwald to the prom because she was from the wrong side of the tracks.

September 14

Here is the text of a letter I sent to the Frito-Lay Corporation earlier this year:

Frito-Lay Inc.
Plano, TX 75235–5224

Dear People at the Frito-Lay Company:

The other day I was eating some of your fine chips. Specifically, I was ingesting Tostitos 100% White Corn BiteSize (did you really mean not to put a space or hyphen in between "Bite" and "Size"?) Perfect for Dipping Chips. I noticed this pseudo-Aztec design bordering the bottom of the bag. I don't know if it was the Sleater-Kinney playing in the background or if I was just feeling particularly proud to be female that day, but it struck me that part of the pseudo-Aztec design looked exactly like a schematic representation of a uterus and

---

*Although Testaverde does not mean "green testicles," as I had hoped.

ovaries. I enclose a photocopy of the chip bag with the stylized uterus and ovaries circled in red, along with a diagram from a medical textbook of an actual uterus and ovaries for comparison.

While some might be disturbed to find female anatomy on their bag of chips, I say "Bravo!" (or perhaps, "Brava!") at your manufacture of such an obviously gynocentric snack product. Is this a shout-out to the craving of many menstruating women for salty snack foods? Or perhaps a subtle Native American influence, an acknowledgment of the Corn = Earth = Earth Mother equation? Whatever the cause, I may say with certainty that I like the result. Long may the uterus reign on my bag of chips.

Jolly good show!

Mimi Smartypants

Her address, etc.

I got a coupon from them and a very generic letter thanking me for enjoying the chips. No reply to my content at all.

← *September 16*

You know that I would never poke fun at homeless crazy people, right? Well okay, yeah, I would. But you have to understand the spirit in which it is done. Part of me of course wishes that there weren't any homeless crazy people. It would be particularly grand if we could do away with the "homeless" part. And if one's mental illness causes one pain and distress (unlike mine, which causes me nothing but *good times*!), then obviously that's not right. But I have to say that many of the crazy street people whom I encounter in Chicago are crazy with flair and style, and seem either to be enjoying themselves or at least so deep in their delusions as to sort of constitute an entirely other universe of their own. They are not of our world. And thus it is not exploitation or a cheap shot if I document these individuals here, for the enlightenment and possible enjoyment of others.

(My constant need to explain myself will probably be the death of me. Or rather it will be the life of me, because if I ever get too close to suicide I think about how people would talk about me behind my back, and I would get no chance to respond, and that would just anger me. You can leave a suicide note but that's no good because everyone would have different reactions to the note; their dialogue is ongoing and yours has ended. There's a bit of a sick-and-wrong and extremely depressing moral in there somewhere, about how life is one long rebuttal to the persuasive whisper of death, or about how a selfish bitch like me continues to walk the planet just so she can get the last word in, but it doesn't do to examine that too closely, does it? Because frankly, we've had a few drinks tonight.)

Crazy homeless people with flair and style. Right. There was a man hanging out by the Sears Tower the other day who was wearing construction boots tied around his neck like ice skates and who was busy shouting out baseball statistics at everyone. One side of his face was pretty sunburned but not the other. However, the best crazy homeless person with flair and style ever hangs out by the IBM building. He is a young black guy with a long, pointy beard. He wears a shower cap and a suede fringed jacket and has a *huge* falconry-style black leather armband (wrist to elbow, seriously) with two-inch metal spikes all over it. Today he had about four beef jerky sticks stuck in his mouth like straight pins, and he was sort of moaning and grunting through his beefy harmonica. (Wow, that sounded dirty. Trust me, it's not at all sexy in person. Intriguing, maybe, from about fifty yards away or at a brisk walking pace. But not sexy.)

⟵ *September 18*

You know what's worse than movies? Theater. Specifically, big-budget Broadway theater where they take a Disney movie and make a play out of it. Or when some horrible old movie musical is adapted for the stage (apparently both *Fame* and *Saturday Night Fever* have recently been made into stage plays. Why? she asks, weeping and rending her garment. Why god, why?). Or a lot of rhythmic stomping for thirty-two dollars a ticket, or that creepy Irish dance thing where people flail their legs around like puppets. Or an Andrew Lloyd Webber monstrosity wherein a bunch of buttmunches on roller skates pretend that they are trains. I mean really. Are you so desperate for entertainment that this is *okay* with you? I seriously would rather eat paste than prostitute my brain by sitting through all that Broadway crap.

Mmmm, paste.

← *September 19*

Oh happy day! There is a chicken living in my alley!

I shit you not. There is definitely a chicken (actually, probably a rooster, but I prefer to call all chickens chickens, regardless of sex) living in one of the garages in my alley. I've been getting to work very early these days, and as I walk down the alley to the bus stop the chicken (rooster) makes a wonderful classic rooster sound, such as one would hear on a sound effects record or one of those children's animal-sound toys. I'm not sure which building the Chicken Garage belongs to, and I have a feeling it is somewhat illegal to keep a chicken in one's garage in the City of Chicago, but there's no way I would ever rat them out because the fact that I live in such close proximity to a real live chicken (rooster) fills me with indescribable joy.

Hey, you take your indescribable joy where you can find it.

← *September 20*

I forgot to wear a bra today. I just, how you say, plumb forgot. This was not the hugest crisis, nor did it spark an international incident. I say that in case some of you adult women out there might be thinking, "What would happen if I didn't wear a bra today?" The answer is: nothing special.

Of course, not wearing a bra for me is no big deal, and is not even terribly titillating (heh heh, she said titillat-

ing) because, as they say in seventh grade, I am a char-
ter member of the Itty-Bitty Titty Committee and thus
have not much need for an Over-the-Shoulder Boulder
Holder.

I did, however, make the mistake of joking about this
bralessness to this guy at work whom I sort of flirt with, in
that sad-ass way that married people flirt when they know
the flirting will safely go nowhere. I could see by the
slightly bug-eyed look that he got that he had no idea
about my lack of bosom support, and that while he was not
turned on by my breasts per se, he was sort of turned on by
the *idea* of my braless breasts, if that makes any sense at all,
and I was sorry the minute the words left my mouth since
it was clearly the wrong thing to say, and now I am probably going to get brought up on sexual harassment charges
or something.

◄── *September 21*

My adventure-packed journey home:

First, my mind was somewhere else and I was sick of
waiting for the #147 express bus so I got on the #151,
which ends up at the same place, only I forgot that the
#151 does not go "express" in any way, but rather mean-
ders up Sheridan forever taking its own sweet time.

Second, I was quite disturbed by the sight of the guy in
front of me eating specific words out of a piece of paper:
he'd hold it in his hand (it looked like a direct-deposit pay
stub) and like a mouse bite out his name, his address, the
totals, etc., chewing and swallowing those bits, and leaving

ragged wet holes. I thought, Why not just destroy the whole thing, if you're worried that someone will find your personal information once you throw it away? Why not just shred it or tear it up into tiny, tiny pieces? Perhaps there was something talismanic about it. A modern-day Sin Eater.

Third, when I finally did get up north and to the place I catch the next bus home, I was hit by a car. Here's what happened: I saw the Devon bus up ahead, and the light was green for me to cross (okay, the DON'T WALK sign was flashing, but the light was still green), so I ran across the road, not quite at the crosswalk (okay, again) and a car was anticipating the light and did not want to stop or even slow down, and so, well, he hit me. In a sense it was more like I ran into the hood of his car, but really, he shouldn't have been going so fast just because the light was *about* to turn in his favor, so I feel he was at fault. (I would, though, wouldn't I? I'm such a princess sometimes.) I'm fine: I bruised my elbow and my hip, and felt shaky and strange when I realized that if I had lost my footing I would definitely have been run over by multiple cars. But other than that: fine.

Fourth, after all that trauma I still missed the bus.

Fifth, I got a cab the rest of the way home and the driver was very articulate and we had a grand old time complaining about politics and the Chicago Transit Authority and all kinds of other stuff, and he got me home cheaply and efficiently, and at some point while I was paying him he lets it slip that he's only been in this country nine days, and I thought that was hilarious because you can't get a taxi license in nine days, so it was obviously a friend or relative's cab and he was driving it around illegally. But he seemed like a nice guy, so I won't tell if you won't.

← *September 22*

I hate making generalizations about the differences between men and women. It's so retro and stupid and it seems to be a favorite topic of bad stand-up comics, and if that's not a reason to hate something, then I don't know what is. That said, I couldn't help observing something odd the other day: LT has been working from home a lot, and a while back when I came home he was quite proud of some things he had done around the house, one of which was to paint our metal kitchen garbage can. "Doesn't it look better now?" he asked me, and I had to admit it did. Painting the metal kitchen garbage can would never have occurred to me in a million years, however. If I was scouting about for domestic improvement projects, I probably would have picked something very prosaic like scrubbing the bathroom or cleaning out the cabinets. Does this point to a failure of imagination on my part? Or a lack of attention to the everyday details on his? Or should I stop reading Deep Meaning into every part of my life and just quit while I'm ahead? (I think I know the answer to this one.)

A funny urban moment: I'm walking across Michigan Avenue and some guy in a giant SUV (because Michigan Avenue is quite the rugged terrain, you know) is trying to make a right turn, and of course he's only paying attention to the traffic coming from his left and none whatsoever to the *pedestrian directly in front of him.* So he's inching up and inching up and coming close to running me over so I thump on his giant SUV hood to warn him to watch it. Then he becomes irate, rolls down the window, and yells, "Fuck you!"

"No, fuck you!" I yell back. (Eloquent, aren't I? But hell, he started it.)

But he has to get the last word in. As he makes his turn, he leans out the window and shouts, "Go back to Mexico!"

Um . . . okay. . . . but I think they'll be rather surprised to see me. Since I have never been there.

⟵ September 27

I had high tea at the fancy-schmancy, five-star, Drake Hotel with my mother a few days ago. I appreciate the Drake for its history and all, but it is very hard on the eyes. The chandeliers, the swirly patterned carpets. The marble, the cherubs, the gilt. The trompe l'oeil ceiling effect. The frightening Chicago matrons who seriously must get up before dawn to begin applying their eye makeup. The Drake Hotel looks like Henry V and Liberace moved in together. (And what a wacky sitcom that would be!) I can see why Saudi princes like to stay there; it reminds them of home.

At work, this week has been one narrowly averted publishing disaster after another. I did not literally have to yell, "Stop the presses!" but it was really close. Medical editing is fun and all, but I can't wait to go home and *not* have to read and edit a stack of technical articles about the gene predisposing to bowel cancer, or pacify an irate chief editor about some imaginary screw-up in last month's issue, or sweet-talk a hollow-eyed and harried page layout person into doing this super-rush job for me, ahead of everything else, please, just this once, I appreciate it so much.

← *September 30*

Very busy, a touch stressed and manic, deadlines looming (looming, I say) around every corner, but with all this running around I get opportunities to practice one of my favorite stress-relieving activities, and for once it's not the one called Big Huge Glasses of Wine: when things get crazy at work I like to practice my kung fu kicks in the elevator. When no one else is in there, of course—I am not (yet) in the habit of going kung fu on the asses of unsuspecting coworkers. I shared my stress relief technique with a friend of mine, who works in building services for the Sears Tower, and he said amusedly, "You know, there most likely are security cameras in that elevator. Most office buildings built after 1990 have them." Oh well. I guess I don't mind too much if there's a lot of security camera footage of me doing kung fu kicks in the elevator. Elevator Girls Gone Wild, tonight on Fox.

← *October 3*

I got a brief chance to feel on the large side this morning, as I was walking up the subway stairs right behind one of Those Girls. You know, those girls with the hair? And the fingernails? And the Ass Pants? So her ass is pretty much right in front of me, all snug in the stretchy Ass-Pant fabric, and this ass is tiny. I have seen baked goods bigger than her ass. Her ass is pathetically small and wan, like an orphan selling matches in the snow. *Where? Is? Your? Ass?* I wanted to cry aloud to the heavens, shaking my fists. I am not a large person but even I have more booty than that.

⟵ October 6

I'm suffering from that small sadness that wafts up in the evenings, like an odor rising up out of the drain. (If the sadness is the odor, what would be the drain? The soul? Quick, someone dump a box of baking soda into my soul!) Last night I went out to dinner with friends, and then back to someone's apartment for drinks. At one point Mark set his digital camera on a tripod and took some photos of the party (which was much less intrusive than it sounds; I barely noticed and I'm pretty self-conscious about such things), and then later hooked the camera up to the television to show the pictures. It was a postmodern walk down memory lane, a little slide show of how the party looked fifteen minutes ago. Ah, we were all so young then!

⟵ October 7

A thought (which may or may not be useful or true; you be the judge): all serious, "real" friendship is a tiny bit erotically charged. This comes through most clearly in grade school. I was never "popular" but was more the type to have one intense best friend with whom I did everything—having sleepovers; engaging in elaborate, complicated playground games; writing ten-page letters whenever we were forced to be separated by things like summer camp. And if we ever got in a fight, there were dramatic scenes and tears and passionate apologies, just like lovers in some Italian opera.

Of course, you grow up and your friends become a bit more utilitarian: this is the girl I see punk bands with, this is the boy I can call on a weeknight for a beer, this is the girl who laughs at everything I say (always good for an ego boost), this is the colleague I can talk football with, this is the friend who will let me send a maudlin e-mail at 3 A.M. and not tease me about it later. But think about it: with your very closest friends, isn't there still that little spark of attraction? You love the shape of her mouth, you love to watch her smoke, and she says such interesting things. He lets you make outrageous double entendres and naughty jokes, and it's safe because nothing romantic is going to happen between you. Having a close friend allows for non-goal-oriented flirting, which is good for the soul. *Thus spake Mimi Smartypants.*

Today I've been nibbling all day, rather than eating proper meals, and I just realized I've been alternating the sweet and the salty: banana, rice cake, dried fruit, instant vegetarian "chicken" soup, oatmeal cookie, Wheat Thins. Who cares? Right. Moving on.

October 10

THE FOLLOWING IS REALLY GROSS AND I APOLOGIZE FOR THAT

I am a tea drinker. I am forgetful. That makes me a forgetful tea drinker. I have three tea receptacles in my office: one big steel industrial-looking travel mug with the company logo, one ceramic mug with an elephant on it, and another travel mug featuring the Powerpuff Girls. Having this many teacups, in combination with the forgetfulness, is bad news. Especially with travel mugs, since they have those lids, and I tend to put them on the windowsill when I am through without realizing that there is still some tea left inside. Can you see where this is going? Yesterday I grabbed one of the mugs to go wash it out, and what slithered out in the sink was not to be believed. Mold, when it forms on leftover Twinings Irish Breakfast tea, can be a solid, rubbery disk about four inches across. My mold blob actually managed to stop up the sink. I had to take a deep breath and reach in there with a wad of paper towels to get rid of it. Then I scrubbed my hands raw with the hottest possible water, like I was undergoing nuclear decontamination, and washed and washed and washed the mug, and tried to put the horror behind me. I have now taped a note to each of my tea mugs that says, WASH ME OR FACE THE RUBBERY MOLD DISK.

⟵ *October 11*

Sometimes life is full of such whimsical shit. LT and I had a discussion last night about why the clock got combined with the radio, to form the clock radio. (Hi. Still with me? Clock + radio = clock radio.) ("Clock radio" is such a fun phrase to say. Try it in sort of a high-pitched Johnny Rotten/Jello Biafra strained punk-rock whine, using a big fat permanent marker as a makeshift microphone: clock clock clock clock clock clock *radio*!) (I totally just got caught doing just that in my office. Whoops.)

Where was I? Oh. Anyway, we decided that two can play at this game, Mr. Clock Radio, and invented some other combination appliances. But since it's funnier if the appliances don't work very well, I bring you:

1. The combination hair dryer and phone. (*What? I can't hear you! What?*)

2. The combination toaster oven and electric razor. (Oh, this is really dangerous. Melted cheese that close to your face? Plus the grotesque-but-inevitable little tiny hairs in your Hot Pocket or veggie burrito. Ewwww.)

3. The combination microwave and heating pad. (This would be kind of cool, actually, because you could be lying around with cramps and the heating pad on you and be making a tasty snack at the same time! But I don't think enough is known yet about microwaves to trust them so close to your internal organs.)

4. The combination garlic press and hot glue gun. (Oh, what a mess.)

5. The combination bread machine and hamster exercise wheel. (Now you really are just asking for trouble.)

⟵ *October 14*

I have trouble with a lot of things at the beginning of the week. I have trouble with gross motor coordination, with simple addition, with remembering why it's at all important that I get to work on time, and with trying not to feel all mopey like a sad neglected muffin growing stale on the bakery shelf. (The title of my mopey muffin memoir: *I Am Lemon Poppyseed* by Mimi Smartypants.) The easy way out is to talk about my weekend, but I'm so damn boring that there's not much to talk about. Friday I went out for "a few" (by which I mean many) drinks with Kat, and we ruled the jukebox with all our semi-ironic nostalgia tunes. Topics of conversation included the irrational hatred we feel for Michael Jackson; how difficult it is to find genuine unmediated spiritual experiences; how the only song that we really want to strip to onstage is AC/DC's "Back in Black"; irritating pseudo feminism; and group dynamics (the more people you get together in a room, the less likely it is that anything will actually get done). Then we went to a different bar, had more drinks, and I lost a few more arm-wrestling matches.* See? *I am so predictable.* I think I need a hobby.

---

*Why are there so few female arm-wrestling combatants? Come on, ladies! Look at me and my Muppet-like spaghetti arms! I can do you no harm!

⟵ *October 18*

Funniest instant message ever: Kat pops up in my window (my virtual, computer-based window: we are not regulars on *Hollywood Squares* or anything), asking, "How do you make a salmon loaf?" Now, thinking fast is my specialty. I assume this must be one of those riddles, like "How Much Does A Grecian Urn?" "Overpay it and give it high-speed Internet access at work?" I reply, which totally baffles Kat, who simply wanted to know if I had any insights into how to use up some canned salmon, because when she is not working she is drinking or watching *Buffy the Vampire Slayer*, and thus she can't be bothered to do proper grocery shopping and has a tendency to eat like a refugee. (Cue the Tom Petty: Don't! Have! To Eat Like a Refugee!) How do you make a salmon loaf? (Insert your own punchline here.)

⟵ *October 21*

Do you remember when there was a one-to-one correlation with an event and feeling sad? When you fell off your bike, you got sad. When you found out that most of your class thought you were a huge dork and that they hated you for getting good grades, you got sad. But now there is one big amorphous blob of sad. Only occasionally is there the direct correlation. Like the time, embarrassingly recently, when LT found me in front of the television weeping at some nature special about the hippopotamus. This hippopotamus and her baby had to walk and walk forever to find some water, and hippos don't walk very well for long distances so that was a struggle, and then when they finally got to the watering hole it was full of elephants who tried to beat her up and chase her away, but she got all hippo-rageful and stood her hippo ground while her baby hippo drank water, and for some reason the whole thing just made me very sad. Hippo sad.

⟵ *October 26*

At lunch I went out for sushi and the waitress talked to me as if I were a wild animal. This sushi waitress leaned way over my table and asked very softly and gently and compassionately if she could bring me anything to drink, and then when she set down my green tea very gently she gave me a sad smile like "you poor thing," and her manner was so careful and delicate that I thought she might follow up her recitation of the specials with the news that I had terminal cancer. I hope she is like this to everybody and it's not that I look particularly dangerous or unhinged today.

⟵ *October 28*

**LIST OF INTRIGUING TRASH IN MY ALLEY
THIS MORNING, FOR REAL, WHY WOULD I LIE**

Two toilets, one white, one pink
A giant sock (really big husky-sized sock)

Some sort of hockey-based board game
Incredibly ugly lamp, no shade
Broken menorah (looks like it was run over by a car)
Empty box for a snack cake called Raisin Cream Pies
   (doesn't that sound vile?)
Birdcage, no bird inside
Baby carrier, no baby inside
Computer monitor
Hideous brown and yellow afghan; was that yarn on sale
   or something?
Styrofoam head for holding wigs, which I almost took
   but it would have been awkward on the train

The sight of the Styrofoam head briefly made my heart
beat faster because from a distance all I could see was
that it was head-shaped. Maybe you didn't know this,
but I would really love to find a human head. Sometimes
it seems like everyone has found a human head but me.
Yeah, it would be grisly, but I look at medical photographs all day long; I could handle it. Think how long
you could drink on this story! Everyone would be all
like, "Tell us again about how you found the head!"
"Well," I'd say, wiggling around on the barstool to get
more comfortable, "I was just walking down the alley
minding my own business when I noticed this blood-
stained pillowcase . . ."

Of course, eventually people would get sick of hearing
the head story. They would tactfully excuse themselves to
use the bathroom when you started telling it again, or they
would try and change the subject, and eventually your best
friend would be blind drunk one night and would just

burst out with "God! Can you shut up about that head already!" and you'd be all like, "Ha ha, sorry" but on the inside your feelings would be really hurt. I mean, he didn't have to *yell* at you like that.

That's when you start looking for a torso.

As long as we are talking of disturbing things, on this morning's El ride I was not even able to practice my usual Commuting Routine of reading or constructing elaborate baroque orgiastic fantasies in my head. (Casts of dozens! Interesting geometric furniture! Clouds of opium smoke! Everyone's bisexual!) The reason I could not concentrate on these things was the loud and intrusive conversation going on to the left of me, and I use the word "conversation" loosely because it really was more of a diatribe delivered by a loud woman with a serious South Side accent and all the accompanying vocal tics (such as "you know what I'm saying?" after every sentence).

She leads off with the weather. Damn, it's cold. And so forth. This eventually switches to a rant about the bastards who towed her car because she parked in a towaway zone for ten minutes! Can you believe it! (Yes. I can.) Then there was how much money it cost her to get her car back. Then there was a discussion about how she considered going to law school, and took a couple of law classes at City College, but then realized that she'd have to sell her soul in order to drive a Mercedes-Benz. (Because of course, there is no middle ground in the law, like actually helping people or anything like that. Lawyer = soulless rich bastard, period.) (I don't often find myself defending lawyers, but I hate illogic.) Then a rant about the legal system in general, and how public defenders always tell you to plead guilty. For instance, twenty years ago when she shot her boyfriend. (I start listening a little harder right about now.)

(The following is transcribed from my notebook.)

Loud Woman: I shouldn't have been messing with him anyway, because he was a married man, but hell! That ain't my problem! *I* wasn't married to him! You know what I'm saying? I was dealing at the time. My boyfriend, he was trouble, but I loved him so much. He spent the night, and we had relations, you know what I'm saying? Then I wake up and he is gone, and so is my money. Thirty-five dollars. It wasn't the money, but the principle of the thing, you don't *take* shit from me. You just don't. If I got something you want, just ask, but don't *take* from me. So I got my .38, and I went over to his house, and his wife is all up in my face, saying "He wasn't with you last night, get out of here," and I say, "Oh yes he was, bitch, why don't you smell him? He was with me, go ahead, smell him." I didn't mean to shoot him. I just wanted my money, but he looked so damn smug, and then he started to come out the door, and in my mind he was getting ready to hit me, so I shot him in the kneecap. Then I stood there until the cops showed up.

Then her rant about the justice system resumed, about how the asshole public defender told her to plead guilty, why would he do a thing like that? (Um . . . because you were?) The boyfriend declined to press charges (aww, true love!) so she never did any time. Later she got mad at him again for some other reason so she went over to his house and "fucked up his truck real good with a brick and a two-by-four." The best part of this entire urban storytelling episode was that the guy she was telling it to seemed sincerely interested, and when I got off the train they were exchanging phone numbers.

⟵ October 29

During the first daylight-savings *fall back* commute home, on the El, dark at 5:30 in the evening, scooting past everyone's lighted windows, and these two contradictory (and yet not contradictory) emotions:

1. The feeling of chugging past all these fleeting glimpses of butter-yellow domesticity, the couches, the murmuring televisions, the kitchen tables, the pots on the stove, the laughing babies in their playpens, the lamps, the vases of flowers, the bookcases, and you wish that instead of sitting there with freezing cold hands, sandwiched in between The Smelliest Man Alive and The Woman Who Won't Stop Yakking on Her Cell Phone, you were turning the key in the lock of one of these warm apartments and smelling the simmering of something tomato-based, and someone would hand you a baby with its clean little head and footed pajamas, and your life would be sort of like fainting into a featherbed, no terrible drill-bit thoughts ahead of you, each day separate and entire.

2. Alternatively and just as pleasurable: from your privileged position at the train window, the Ultimate Outsider, you can find these scenes of cozy domestic bliss stifling and repugnant, and you can feel a bit otherworldly and cruel and, yes, let's admit it, unjustly superior, with your hard-edged cynical thoughts and your shopping bag full of Difficult Books. You are the giant crow shrieking doom and holding knowledge under your bird claws like a telephone wire, because this is you, out here in the cold, your destination still quite a ways away, and these deluded saps with their babies and their casseroles will never know it. And you can catch a glimpse of yourself in the reflected mirror, your eyes huge and lemurlike and a bit smeared by clumsy eyeliner, and your hair escaping from its messy bun like the Lady of Shalott (half sick of shadows), and you can wonder if that's what you really look like or just what you look like when it gets dark too early.

Then you will finally arrive home and maybe there will be something simmering on the stove, and someone or some cat is glad to see you, and even if not it is still immensely satisfying to let yourself in and be alone in a place and think, "I am here now," no longer in transit but arrived. Not to mention the fact that you have gotten away from The Smelliest Man Alive, unless you have invited him home, in which case I can't help you.

⟵ October 30

I am still going deaf, but I continue to mishear things in lovely and creative ways, so I do not mind one bit. Just keep talking nice and loud and allow me to think you are more interesting or funny than you actually are. This past weekend I was watching football and folding laundry, and the announcers were doing one of those dead-time plugs for other shows on the network, which are super-annoying because I cannot effectively zap that kind of advertising through the magic of TiVo. The play-by-play guy said something about "the hottest new drama on television," called *Cold Case*. In my deafness I thought he said *Coffeecake*. But sadly there is no dramatic television series called *Coffeecake*, although there should be. In the pilot episode, Bob brings a coffeecake to work and puts it in the breakroom. It's . . . caramel pecan! And everyone stands around looking all stricken, like on *ER*, and the lights are all dim like on *West Wing*, and maybe it's raining outside. *Coffeecake*, tonight at eightsevencentral.

LT is going deaf too. In the car I was telling him about my next homemade T-shirt, which is going to say, GEE YOUR HAIR SMELLS IRONIC, and he thought I had said, GEE YOUR HAIR SMELLS LIKE RAMEN. I decided to make that one as well, in his size because he thought of it.

◄— *October 31*

I sent LT out to buy beer and he came back with beer and a pumpkin. I have not carved a pumpkin in years, and I confess I didn't have a lot to do with the carving of this one, except for a bit of help with scooping out the goop. LT, on the other hand, sliced up that gourd like he graduated from an accredited four-year Gourd-Slicing College. "You're the Gourdmaster," I said. "You totally mastered that gourd." We stuck it in the window, with candles, just like you are supposed to (got to give some light to all those wandering dead souls). I went to bed before he did and when he came in I woke up a bit and asked, "Did you extinguish the gourd?" and he said, "You sure are getting a lot of mileage out of that word tonight."

I think a multicultural Klansman costume would be cool for Halloween. You could make the pointy hood out of kente cloth and stitch a yarmulke to the top. Wear one of those Africa medallions plus some rainbow beads and a big pink triangle badge. Greet everyone with "Salaam alaikum, my Aryan brothers!" And the chance of running into any real KKK members would be small. I bet they don't think much of Halloween, since it is not about Jesus, and they get enough dressing up during their stupid rallies and such.

⟵ November 3

Oh, pants. Today. Today is no good. Here is why.

1. Today I managed to spill boiling water all over my foot. I was wearing an insulating shoe, so no injuries were sustained, but still. I have at my desk an Illegal Electric Teakettle (shhhh). Having an electric teakettle is against the rules at my office, because my office building has some mistaken notion that I do not drink tea all day, and that every time I want to have some tea I also want to get up and go all the way down to the cafeteria. Because I have no electrical outlets at human height, the Illegal Electric Teakettle is way underneath my desk, on the floor (which I guess conveniently also helps to hide its illegality), and thus I have to crawl around on the floor to make tea. So very dignified, especially on important-meeting days when I am wearing a suit. Today I got all cocky first thing in the morning and thought I could just reach down to the floor and pour the boiling water into my teacup, only you know what? It helps if you actually look and take note of where the teacup *is* before you start to pour the boiling water, because then you might notice that you are about twelve inches away from the cup and you are, in fact, pouring boiling water on your shoe.

2. Today is also the day that proves I really am going deaf, because I thought that my boss had just walked into my office and called me a "fascist twat." I was quite taken aback but it turned out to be some innocent work-related statement.

━ *November 4*

THE FUNNY-ONLY-TO-US CHAT TRANSCRIPT

mimismartypants: From *A New Booke of Cookerie*, published in 1615, I shall quote: "Then worke it stiffe like a pudding, and cram it in againe."

Tom: Whoa. I like to cram it in the pudding.

mimismartypants: It's the hottest cookbook sentence ever. Part of the hotness is the spelling.

mimismartypants: Worke it stiffe like a pudding.

mimismartypants: That sentence is about making some stuffing to stuff inside a swan.

mimismartypants: Cram it in the swan againe.

mimismartypants: "Ahhh, go cram it in the swan."

mimismartypants: "I enjoy anal, three-ways, and swan-cramming."

Tom: With a stiffe pudding.

Tom: Swan cramming. I should make a Craigslist personal for that.

mimismartypants: It's a fantastic insult too. "Go cram it in the swan." Particularly with a Chicago accent.

Tom: I bet Asian fetishists would be turned on by the phrase "swan cramming."

mimismartypants: "When all is boyled well together, put in your Fish, and scum it well."

mimismartypants: The authors keep using that possessive for food: "parboyle your legge." "Put in your Fish."

Tom: Wait, you cram the swan with a fish?

mimismartypants: Sorry, this is a different recipe.

mimismartypants: "To hash a Legge of Mutton in the French fashion."

mimismartypants: "To make an Vmble Pye, or for want of Vmbles to doe it with a Lambes head and Purtenance."

mimismartypants: What the fuck? I can't decipher that one.

Tom: Humble? Umble. Vmble.

mimismartypants: I thought humble pie had no meat, though. If you have no humble, use a lamb's head?

mimismartypants: If you have hubris, use a lamb's head.

Tom: And purtenance.

mimismartypants: "Stampe it in a Morter till it come like Paste, all in a lumpe."

Tom: The head?

mimismartypants: No, new recipe again . . . the buttocke of a wilde Boare.

Tom: Elizabethan cookbooks vs. Mike Tyson's press conferences. Much the same syntax.

mimismartypants: "Cram It in The Swan Againe" by AC/DC.

Tom: No replies to the swan-cramming ad yet.

mimismartypants: Come on, swan-crammers.

Tom: I thought Chicago was full of swan-crammers.

mimismartypants: We could start a LiveJournal community.

Tom: Yes. Of two people.

mimismartypants: That's the best kind of LiveJournal community.

mimismartypants: "Cramming the swan" could also be anything, really. A skateboard term.

Tom: A financial term. Secret Enron e-mails about Operation Swan Cram.

mimismartypants: Swanny McSwanCram.

mimismartypants: Delicious Crammed Swan.

Tom: We could bring it back as a vegan dish: "It's really yellow peppers simmered in coconut milk. We just call it a crammed swan."

mimismartypants: A seitan swan, crammed with leeks.

mimismartypants: Here's another good part: "Then have ready the Greate Gutts of Mutton."

Tom: That's so like a directive from some hobbit-rock song.

mimismartypants: Greate bigge globs of greesy grimie gophere gutts.

Tom: Geddy Lee singing:

Tom: "Then have ready the Greate Gutts of Mutton/For when the swan come to cramme you . . ."

mimismartypants: Now I'm all laughing in my office.

Tom: And your head is smashed into a paste.

mimismartypants: Come! Like Paste! All! In! A Lumpe!

⟵ *November 5*

I got to go out last night and listen to music and drink cheap sleazy beer, in a sensible and grown-up fashion that made me all proud of myself. Count along with me:

1. There is no such thing as one beer. Well, maybe there is, if you are out with your parents for Indian food or something. But other than that, one beer does not exist.

2. Two beers. Two beers is what you say you had when you are *lying.* "I only had two beers." Right. Of course you did. Liar.

3. Then we come to the paragon of righteousness, the guardian of your untroubled deep-REM sleep, Mr. Thirdbeer. Mr. Thirdbeer is a truly good citizen. With Mr. Thirdbeer you feel safe and protected. You have a proper little buzz on, but you can go home right now, have a nice conversation with your husband, watch a little TV, drink a little water just for the hell and hydration of it, and climb into bed like the safe, sane, healthy, non–problem drinker that you are. (Note: this is where I was at last night. Yay for me, all sensible on a weekday.)

4. Did you know that Mr. Thirdbeer has an evil twin? Not many people do. His name is Prince Plastered the

Fourth. Welcoming this dark prince into your evening greatly increases the chances that you will hear the words *"Last Call,"* and then you will be making like David Byrne: "Well? How did I get here?"

5. Why? Because Prince Plastered the Fourth, being royalty, never travels alone. He has many courtiers and hangers-on, like Footman Fifthbeer and Little Lord Cuervo Shot.

← *November 7*

There is a rumor afoot that at the house where I will be spending Thanksgiving (the in-laws), ham, and not turkey, will be served. This had better not be true. I don't even eat turkey but I am a staunch traditionalist in this area. And does ham equal no stuffing? There goddamn better well be stuffing. If not, I shall be polite and gracious at first, but after a bunch of wine I may begin to make pointed remarks. Perhaps I shall drink a bunch of wine and make pointed remarks anyway; that sounds like fun. Of course, were it up to me we'd all eat massive amounts of vegetarian Indian food for Thanksgiving. I would volunteer to carve the giant dosa.

← *November 9*

ONCE UPON A TIME THERE WERE SOME WINDOWS

1. When I was very small my bedroom window looked out onto another apartment building where my best friend lived. We always wanted to rig up some sort of communi-cation device across the gangway but we never did. She had long pigtails with bangs like me, and her mom once shocked me by serving Kraft macaroni and cheese with sliced hot dogs mixed in throughout.

2. In our next place I had a corner room with unexciting views of the side and back yards. Sometimes there would be the horrible view of our overweight neighbor, a truly despised French teacher at the Catholic high school, per-forming some shirtless yardwork. Have you ever seen grass clippings stuck to fat rolls on a French teacher's sweaty back? Lucky you.

3. One of my college rooms had this tiny suicide-proof sliding window that looked onto a slope of sorts. I hesitate to call it a "hill," but it was relatively steep for the mid-western prairie and good for some minor sledding in the winter.

4. Another college place had a fabulous corner bedroom with six windows. A huge pine tree tapped against one of the windows all night, every night, and during a few mental-health-unfriendly postmidnight hours, stoned on loneliness and unproductive abstract thoughts, I remember opening the window and touching the pine needles, just for the comfort of something actual and organic. A tree is a fact you can learn, like multiplication.

5. I once lived in a room with only one window, but that led out onto a part of the roof that was very nice to sit on. One night, who knows how it started, all the occupants of that house ended up sitting out there naked. There was this beautiful boy named Eric living in town that summer, and he came over that evening and started to crawl out to the roof to join the party, and someone said in warning, "Hey, Eric . . . uh, we're all naked out here." "Oh, no problem," he said, shucked off all his clothes, and continued through the window.

6. One of my apartments in Hyde Park had only one set of windows in the living room that looked out onto a small shopping plaza across the street. A few weeks after I moved in, someone was murdered at the shopping plaza pay phone, the pay phone I had been using to call my mother while the phone company took their sweet time getting our service connected, and I mistakenly mentioned this to her in a slice-of-life-urban-anecdote way and she was decidedly not amused.

7. In Bahrain, in the apartment we lived in during LT's PhD fellowship, my bedroom window looked out onto a vast waste of reclaimed land. Sometimes there were feral dogs trotting around out there. In the distance were palm trees and some mosque minarets, and the winter sunsets were occasionally travel-poster gorgeous, with the sounds of overlapping muezzins calling people to prayer in the background.

8. Another Chicago apartment had a very poorly fitted bedroom window. Terrible drafts blew right in and daylight could be seen around the cracks. One winter Sunday LT and I woke up to blizzard conditions *inside* the bedroom and a small snowdrift accumulating on the windowsill and floor. I suppose this could have been construed as ghetto-depressing but it was actually kind of cozy and funny. LT brought me clothes so I could get dressed under the quilts and stay warm and then we had pancakes.

9. There were other apartments but none with remarkable views or window stories. My current place has nice, basic, rehabbed windows. Last summer the neighbors to the south, visible out our dining room window, cut down some flowering hedges for no reason, which angered LT. He vowed to walk around naked in front of that window for a whole day in protest and to teach them a lesson that privacy hedges are a good thing. Even though I tried to tell him that the neighbors were probably not making the connection between their yardwork and his nudity, he stuck to his plan.

← *November 12*

Why do people not let you know when you have food on your face or your shirt tag sticking out or some other fixable cosmetic problem? There are limits to this mini social contract, of course, the main one being the "fixable" part. If a friend says, "Does my hair look stupid?" or "Are these pants okay?" I will probably automatically say "no" and "yes," respectively, unless we are talking about a devil lock or buttless chaps (again, respectively). But basic stuff like lipstick on the teeth? *Please say something*. Otherwise you will end up like me, and sit through an entire meeting not knowing that you have a large swath of purple ink on your cheek, from your earlier too-emphatic gesturing with an uncapped pen. I wonder if my coworkers thought I had finally gone nuts and was getting all commando with the office warpaint. But wait, it gets worse. I am in the bathroom after the meeting, noticing my purple face streak and crabby that no one mentioned anything all day, when I notice also that I have a section of hair, left side front, that has a big glob of white toothpaste-spit dried on, because apparently after lunch I was not paying attention and brushed messy. So add that to the dazed expression I tend to acquire during stupid business meetings and *I look like a street crazy.* The pen is bad enough, but what kind of spaz spits toothpaste on her own hair? I am going to have to start wearing a ponytail holder on my wrist, to get rid of the hair for things like toothbrushing and blowjobs (hello! good morning, readers! are you awake now?). *Oh god.* Saying that makes me think of another reason why my colleagues may have been reluctant/embarrassed/shy about mentioning my hair issue. *No. Never mind. Let's not go there.*

⟵ November 13

Whenever I am watching football (the game with all the ludicrously huge guys running into each other, not the game with all the sinewy South American guys running past each other: I include this note so as to make this journal thingy internationally comprehensive. That is me, always with the helpfulness.)

I forgot what I was talking about.

Oh. Whenever I am watching football with other people, I like to notice the different styles of talking back to the television. LT tends to punish ignorance rather than reward success: he does not celebrate much at touchdown time but show him a missed tackle or flubbed sack and he gets exasperated. My dad asks rhetorical questions: *"What are you doing? What kind of a play was that?"* And I recently had it pointed out to me (since one does not always have awareness of one's sports-watching behavior) that I tend toward the gentle exhortation of the gentlemen on the screen: "Run, sweetie! Go baby go!"

⸺ *November 14*

Last Wednesday afternoon, I am on the train (*yeah I know I am always on the train what is your point*), feeling very cheerful because it is a sunny day and I got to go home at a reasonable hour, and because LT and I have planned an evening of grilling out and drinking beer (true to gender stereotypes, I am SideDishGirl, he is FireGuy). I have a grocery bag with me. I take an empty seat next to a guy wearing some manner of sports jersey. Middle-aged. Beard. That is pretty much all I remember, and it doesn't even begin to explain what happened next, but there it is.

"What's in the bag?" he asks as soon as I sit down. Now you never know when you are going to run into some Grocery Anthropologist who is doing a ground-breaking study, and remember it is a cheerful sunny day, so I answer truthfully: dried apricots, wasabi peas, and a cucumber.

"Oh, a *cucumber*," he leers, chuckling assholically. (Is that an adverb? It should be.)

About now is where I give him a fifty-megaton dirty look. I would think twice about unleashing this look even on individuals as reprehensible as Mussolini or Ann Coulter. This was high-octane; I was slightly shocked that such a blistering, no-holds-barred dirty look could come out of my eyes. If looks could kill, break out the pus-wiping rags because this dirty look would surely mean Ebola Time. (Ebola Time! Don't touch this! Dope in Zaire, magic in Sudan! Nice pants, Hammer!)*

He reels a bit from the force of the look and says, "Sorry, sorry, I was just joking with you." I don't say anything. "Come on, baby! It was a joke! You know I'm a nice guy, right?" I reply, "Actually, I think you've just proved yourself to be a creep with no social graces whatsoever."

He was nice and quiet for the rest of the ride, and I was free to read my book. My innocent and wholesome groceries nestled at my feet.

— November 16

A BIG THUMBS-UP TO BANAL CONVERSATIONS

At the Loyola El stop, getting off the train:

Guy #1: Want to go to the liquor store?
Guy #2: Yes! Immediately!

---

*Disclaimer: Mimi Smartypants does not actually think fatal hemorrhagic fevers are funny. Well, maybe a little, but just in that If We Don't Laugh, We Will Cry, and Then We Will Start to Scream, and Then We Will End Up Either Permanently Curled in the Fetal Position or Washing Our Hands Every Twenty Seconds way. But linking MC Hammer with Ebola virus was pretty funny, and maybe if the whole MC/DJ dichotomy makes a resurgence there could be MC Ebola and DJ Pustule, from Tha Funkee BioTERRORizm Crew, Yo Yo Yo Auugggh! Featuring the Toxic Foxes and the Anthrax Dancers! Fo Shizzle Smallpoxizzle! (Oh man I have a feeling I didn't do that right. I never claimed to be hip-hop.)

In line at the Walgreens at Clark and Erie:

Baby Momma #1: So I said hello! *Hello!* What the fuck are you talking about? I don't want to take custody of her! I got my own babies to worry about! Shit!

Baby Momma #2: Uh-huh.

Baby Momma #1: But then I was like, Wait. That's *money,* you know? Extra check.

Baby Momma #2: Uh-huh.

In virtual space (I admit to being addicted to instant messaging):

mimismartypants: You know my panhandler rule, right?

ssirilyan: A shiny dollar to the first person who asks for it?

mimismartypants: Right. Then I'm done. I don't always get asked, so then I just transfer the dollar to tomorrow's pocket.

mimismartypants: And I deflect anyone else this way: when someone says, "Spare some change?" I look right at them and say "How's it going?" or "Good morning!" or whatever.

mimismartypants: That seems unusual enough that they are startled, and then I'm already gone.

ssirilyan: I have thought of carrying a hamburger with me. Because if they want to buy food, then I will give them food.

mimismartypants: God that was the best sentence ever out of context.

mimismartypants: I have thought of carrying a hamburger with me.

mimismartypants: I want to sneak it into a Beckett play.

ssirilyan: *falls out of chair laughing*

mimismartypants: Often, at night. I have thought. Of carrying a hamburger with me.

ssirilyan: He said he would carry a hamburger.

mimismartypants: Is it time to carry a hamburger?

mimismartypants: (despairingly) This hamburger is too large. To be carried.

mimismartypants: In the rain.

ssirilyan: You carry my hamburger now. I am weary.

Me and LT, on the phone, from work:

LT: What should I feed you tonight?

Me: Let's go out. Somewhere. So we can talk.

LT: Uh. Do we have things to talk about?

Me: We always have things to talk about!

LT: But, like, *things?*

Me: Oh god no, not *things.* Sorry. No, no. Not like a we-need-to-talk talk.

LT: Not talk talk.

Me: Not talk talk. No British new-wave involved.

LT: What?

Me: Never mind.

LT: Okay.

Me: I'm hungry.

Another good one from this morning: LT and I were sort of making out in the kitchen, even though I had my bag over my shoulder and transit card in my hand and was but moments from missing the bus.

(ear kissing and licking)

Me (cartoony Texas babbling noises): Beebee ba bee. Dabadabada. Hoo-eee.

LT: What was that?

Me: Sorry. That last one turned me into Ross Perot.

LT: Yikes.

◄— November 17

Last night I was walking around cleaning things (sort of), and I had the TV on, and I heard a voice from it ask, "Are you tired of the same old flakes?" Yes, I thought. I am tired of the same old flakes. But why keep this feeling to myself? "I'm tired of the same old flakes," I said out loud. "Hey Cat," I yelled from the bathroom, "I'm tired of the same old flakes!" I don't know why I glommed on to this phrase, but it vastly amused me. LT kind of thought I was losing it.

◄— November 19

Let's hear it for free Internet access from my hotel in Washington, D.C., where I am for a science editors' conference. The guest services booklet claims it's free, but there's a sign next to me in this kiosk (god I love the word "kiosk") that claims it's thirty-five cents a minute. But no one's asked me for a credit card or room number or anything like that. So there!

Saturday night I finally managed to get to sleep in my too-quiet hotel room with its too-soft pillows, only to be woken up at 3:30 A.M. by a fire alarm. I am an incredibly light sleeper, and the alarm woke me up but it didn't heart-attack wake me up, it was more of an annoying presence out in the hotel hallway. Perhaps I have been overly well-trained by all the fire alarm hoaxes in high school and college, because I honestly lay in bed for about thirty seconds, thinking that this had to be a mistake. Then I thought, "Wait. I don't want to be the asshole who dies in a hotel fire because she didn't think the fire alarm was real." So I put on clothes, grabbed my room key, and went outside. I even felt the door first like a real Safety Sam. Outside, the alarm was still shrieking but there was no one in the hallway. I stood there for a minute, and then *one* other sleepy-looking person came out of her room, smiled at me, and headed for the elevator. Well, if we truly had to evacuate I was going to do it by the book, so I started going down the exit stairs (from the twenty-first floor), simultaneously pissed off about the nonemergency this was turning out to be and a little freaked out because going down and down and down fire exit stairs will forever have unpleasant associations after the World Trade Center. When I got to about the ninth floor, the fire alarms suddenly stopped. I stood in the stairway for a while, and since I could hear zero activity and zero sirens I stepped out into the ninth-floor hallway and encountered some other hotel guests, who said that they had called down to the front desk and that it was a false alarm. Okay. It was four in the morning, I had to get up in three hours, but it's better than dying of smoke inhalation or becoming a horrifying clip on the evening news. Back to bed. An entire hour later, drifting off to sleep, there was a knock on my door. Once again I had to get dressed and answer the door (leaving the chain thingy on, since now I'm in full-blown Safety Mode). It was a hotel employee. "Just wanted to tell you there's no fire," he said. "That was just a false alarm, we've fixed the system. Everything's fine." Great, I thought. You woke me up to tell me there is no fire. Keep me posted, please—if there's not an earthquake later, I want to be the first to know.

← *November 20*

If I were writing a science fiction or fantasy novel (which I would never do), I would be very tempted to use only the names of prescription drugs for all the proper nouns. "Once upon a time on the Planet Xanax, near the great Demerol Forest and the river Wellbutrin, King Haldol sat brooding in Castle Vicodin." And so on.

I came in very late to work yesterday. I had a terrible time getting back from Washington D.C., the planes were all stacked up due to some mysterious "bad weather" in Chicago and we circled forever. Circled forever with my loquacious seatmate jabbering in my ear, of course, about rodeos and reptiles and smokers' rights and the superiority of Texas over anyplace else in the world. Literally turning my back to him did not shut him up, pretending to sleep did not shut him up, writing in my notebook did not shut him up, and burying my nose in my book did not shut him up. I regretted not bringing the iPod, with which I could have at least drowned him out. Good god.

←*November 22*

Friday LT and I rode our bikes to Evanston, about five or six miles each way, and had dinner at a Mexican restaurant. He ordered *Pollo Loco*, even though I kept warning him, "That chicken's crazy! That chicken is really quite out of its mind! That chicken has a gun!" It was nice to do something a bit out of the ordinary after work, since I had a crazy week with issues going to the printer and rush rush rush and some sort of plans every single night. I was starting to get a bit strange by Friday. I was calling myself the original editah and asking employees to drop by my "crib" for meetings. Actually, this gangsta/editor might be a fine hip-hop persona for me. I could wear a large gold ampersand around my neck, get a neck tattoo of a pica stick, have William Safire be my beatbox.

←*November 25*

You want events? Fresh, hot, still-dripping-with-grease events? Are you tired of reading diaries where nothing much happens?

Things will happen here, today, in this entry. They may not be interestingly or wittily described, but they will happen.

Ah, Chicago, where we like to drive our trains into each other. It makes for a more exciting commute for LT, who was involved in a crash of two El lines. He suffered no injuries himself, but did end up with a latte-soaked shirt and pants when a couple of Lincoln Park Trixies landed on top of him. Good thing they're always so anorexic or he could have been more seriously injured.

Not to make light of the situation, because many people were seriously injured. LT ended up giving his handkerchief (because he is one of those retro guys who still carries a snot rag) to a man who was bleeding profusely from the face. He (LT, not Mr. Bleeding Face) called me from his cell phone to let me know that yes, he was on the Train of Crashing but that he was fine, thinking that I would hear the news of the accident and be worried, which is a good assumption since I am the queen of worrying. However, I work in a hermetically sealed office building, and outside events do not penetrate. But it was nice of him nonetheless.

So that was Friday, and the city was all a-flurry. Later on Friday Kat called and insisted that I meet her for a drink, and she had that tone in her voice that meant she would soon go after strangers' eyes with a salad fork, and because I am a good friend, I agreed. (Unnecessary note: I really am a good friend. Some people may not think so, because I tend to disappear for days at a time, sometimes I borrow things and sort of forget to give them back, and I will tell you that you are full of shit if, indeed, you are full of shit. You'd be amazed at how many people don't appreciate that. Oh, and I also have this silly diary where I may reveal embarrassing personal details about you. On the plus side, I am loyal, I will always stick up for you in public or private, and if you demand that I meet you for a drink, I will walk over my own grandmother to do so. Just make sure to include the words "for a drink.")

We went out, beers were had, LT eventually joined us

and told funny stories of The Great El Disaster, and some-how, as if by magic, food appeared and was eaten. I love it when that happens. The rest of the weekend was rather uneventful: more food was eaten, live music was heard, and nature shows were watched through the magic of TiVo. Wow. I'm not a gadget girl, but TiVo is a grand thing: the good bits of TV without all the bits that make TV such a cesspool.

This brings us all the way to today, which I spent in the company of junkies, hookers, and thieves: jury duty! The morning started out with a long bus ride down to the jail and courthouse complex at Twenty-sixth and California, a route that takes you through some very interesting (read: ghettotastic) neighborhoods. I saw no fewer than three people up against the hoods of police cars, and it was only nine in the morning. Then through the metal detectors I went, and into the scummy jury room, where I had to fight the urge not to dump bottles and bottles of hand sanitizer all over everything, and where I waited and waited and waited. My number was not called. I read an entire book (luckily I also had a back-up book.) We broke for "lunch." It took me only a quick walk outside, about five blocks in each direction, to determine that there was nowhere to go for lunch. There was a Popeye's Chicken (which for some reason I always read as "Pope Yes Chicken," so that in my mind it is a Catholic chicken place) and a dubious taqueria (it was not literally called "La Trichonosa," but you get my drift). I was propositioned twice on my brief walk outside, and also received an offer to buy a gold chain. I went back in and had some vending machine chips and a bottle of water. Gourmet Day it was not.

At 3 P.M., just when I thought I would get away clean, my number was called and we went to a courtroom for jury selection. We listened to the judge talk about the nature of justice and trial by jury. We listened to people being questioned for jury selection. It was incredibly boring. The lawyers rejected all but four of those people, so then the same thing was repeated with a different batch of people. It took hours, and we weren't allowed to read, so I spent my time covertly making eyes at my defendant. This guy was hot. He may have been an alleged thug (it was a felony weapons charge), but he was an extremely good-looking alleged thug. He had super-high David Bowie cheekbones and a pointy chin and cornrows like Snoop Doggy Dogg. Plus the longest eyelashes I had ever seen on an adult. (It may not sound like the best combination, but trust me, it was nice.) So I guess it's a good thing that I didn't get on the jury, as I may have had some bias there. On the other hand, I was very much looking forward to being questioned because I wanted to tell a small lie in the courtroom. Nothing huge, just that when they asked me what hobbies I had (which for some reason they were asking all the potential jurors), I had planned to say "gardening." A lie, but it hurts no one, and it would give me a thrill to tell a lie in a real live courtroom because I'm a rebel like that.

But no jury duty for me. I collected my $17.20 and made my long journey home.

← *November 29*

My Thanksgiving was totally nonexcruciating. Everyone was normal. I ate a lot of mashed potatoes, as this is not the most vegetarian-friendly day, although my father-in-law rose to the occasion and made a nice couscous thing. The children were cute. Pies had whipped cream on top. So other than the drive out to The Middle of Nowhere, it was fine. We went far enough away from Chicago that the nearest big city is Rockford, they don't have 911, you don't need any special permit to keep some fancy Scottish *cows* (which my father-in-law does), the best pizza in town comes from a gas station, and it is considered perfectly normal to have pieces of rusting farm equipment everywhere. Do I sound prejudiced? I guess I am. The John Cougar Mellencamp lifestyle appeals to me not.

ADDICTION

After the Thanksgiving battle was over, and it had been decided whose cuisine reigned supreme, we drove all the way back to the city and drank the shakes away at my favorite Chicago bar, Delilah's. It has the best light level of any bar in the city (suitable for spelunking), my buddy Foster works hard behind the bar to meet our every booze-related requirement, and they play lots of old-school punk rock, which makes me feel like a kid again. Since Delilah's is open every day of the year, it really should position itself as the post–Family Trauma bar. I have been there after funerals, on Thanksgiving, and I think once on Easter. The staff could give you an armband to wear detailing what event you were there trying to forget (a coffin, a turkey, a bunny) and there would be half-price deals all night. On Thanksgiving, an American holiday, I was in the mood to drink really cheap, evil, American beer. My beer was only a dollar and it said right on the can that it captured the "spirit and strength of America." It was fairly awful but if I drink good beer I think the terrorists win, and Mimi Smartypants stands united. Or maybe she sways united, or slouches united, or sits on your lap all flirty and holiday-tipsy united, but the strength and spirit of America is strong within her.

(I must mention that the spirit and strength of America feels profoundly less spiritual and strong the next day. Ouch.)

◢ *December 1*

There's an "adult bookstore"* near my office that has this sign in the window: LADIES WELCOME. I have two things to say about this: (1) Why, thank you. (2) "Ladies"?

◢ *December 3*

Early this morning the snow started out big. Big snow, real snow, fine fat flakes, the kind of snow that makes you

---

*I just love that term "adult bookstore." Sorry, we don't carry any Michael Crichton here. But we have a lovely copy of *The Brothers Kara-mazov* . . . What? Listen buddy, if it ain't heavy on the symbolism, we don't have it. This is an *adult* bookstore.

proud. You can call up some friend who has just moved to Florida and describe the gorgeous snow scenario and feel smugly superior, because you are a sturdy Midwesterner who's not afraid of a little snow, and now we get to make snow angels and go ice-skating and all kinds of Norman Rockwell things like that. Or at least we have the option. The snow is wide and clean like the future you used to think you would have.

It never lasts. All day the snow has gotten smaller and meaner and sharper and angrier, and there are no *drifting* or even *falling* type of verbs associated with it at this late date. Instead the snow is sort of being thrown sideways and even though you know it is ridiculous to ascribe motives to frozen water, it seems like the snow is after you, and it seems like the snow knows just where the gaps are between glove and sleeve.

— December 4

1. My face hurts from laughing too much.

2. At Delilah's, over beer, last night.

3. Hungover? Not really.

4. Rather, I merely feel a bit polluted. Were I a river, frogs would be mutating in me.

The pollution symptoms:

- The need to hold my head at a strange angle so the thoughts don't spill out.
- Mercifully, I seem to be free of the maroon woolen

blanket of Prufrockian despair that often afflicts me after drinking beer. Perhaps that maroon woolen blanket is in the laundry (instructions on the tag of the maroon woolen blanket of despair: machine wash cold, lay very flat to dry).

- A full-blown Tourette's syndrome–like urge to confess everything. Hopefully I won't be captured by the enemy today, because I'd crack in a second.

- For instance, I was in conference with one of my editors, giving her a glowing performance review, and as I was telling her how valuable a "team member" she is I found myself absurdly close to tears.

- I also welled up a bit on the El when the sunrise skyline heaved (hove?) into view. Somebody please slap me like a hysterical ingénue in an old-timey movie. Get a grip, Ms. Smartypants!

⟵ *December 8*

This morning things were going well. I was enjoying reading the paper and hanging out in my pajamas. And then LT got it in his head that I needed to see *Clash of the Titans*. It had come up a few weeks ago that I had never seen *Clash of the Titans*, and apparently this was some kind of formative movie for LT, since he was astonished and chagrined that I had missed it. So without my knowledge he had TiVo'd a showing of this film, and there it was. Listen to me, and listen well: This. Is. A. Horrible. Movie. I went through the five stages of grief on the couch with this movie.

DENIAL: Okay, it's cheesy. But cheesy can be good. We can laugh at it, right? This could be fun.

BARGAINING: Repeatedly telling LT that I don't want to watch this movie anymore. Him calmly informing me that that's fine, we can stop it and resume tomorrow. He even pauses it when I go to the bathroom, just to make sure I don't miss any *Clash of the Titans* golden moments. Eventually I am allowed to fetch my book, but of course *Clash of the Titans*, with its all-powerful suckiness, filters in, and eventually I just give up.

ANGER: What squadron of ass clowns made this film? It's not just cheesy, clunky, wooden, and bad, it literally makes no sense at times. It employs interminable establishing shots (*Yes we get it. This takes place in a swamp.*) and lazy narrative tricks, like soliloquies where a whole bunch of characters are introduced in turn. And that robot owl! An R2D2 rip-off with none of the charm.

DEPRESSION: (This space intentionally left blank.)

ACCEPTANCE: This movie spans a finite length of time. Soon it will be over and I can go rinse my head in cold water and go take a nap.

Nap I did. Sweet, blessed unconsciousness.

← December 11

My whole El car was preached at yesterday morning. Loudly. And she was a lousy preacher too: no rhythm or timing and very garbled content. (Not that I would appreciate *any* preaching, especially in a confined public space like public transportation. Keep your Jesus to yourself, thanks.) The only good part was this vegetable kick she got on for a while: "You like the *corn*! You like the *carrots*! You like the *eggplant*! You like the *lettuce*! You like the *broc-co-li*! Well, the good Lord made *all* these vegetables for you!"

Crazy Preacher Lady (who had not one but two largish twigs stuck in her hair and a pink quilted ski jacket with JESUS #1! Magic Markered on the back) was relentless, and relentlessly loud, and was on the train with me all the way from the north side to downtown. I did not have headphones or earplugs and I was trying to read while she was shrieking her messages from the Holy Ghost. I suddenly had a vision of leaping up from my seat and beating her to death with a large heavy object, more to just *make the noise stop* than out of any real anger or annoyance. It kind of scared me, since I could really vividly see that scene in my head and since, like I said, there were no accompanying wrathful emotions to go with my violent impulse. Maybe I have vast untapped reservoirs of hidden rage. Maybe I'm a ticking time bomb and don't even know it. If fury were peanuts, I'd be George Washington Carver.

◄━━ *December 15*

I dreamed recently that Bono was breastfeeding a baby and droning on in his Irish Voice of Great Sincerity about how wonderful it was that science had allowed him to experience the miracle of feeding an infant with his own body and how amazing it must be to give birth and blah blah. It was at a party and Bono was wearing all black (even a black nursing bra) and I remember wishing he would shut the hell up.

━ *December 18*

As I scuttled up from the subway with all the other worker beetles, on our way to high-rise offices where we industriously roll dung all day, I saw several large drops of white liquid splatter on the stairs. "Birdshit," I thought. Next, I felt one of these drops land on my head. "Ah," I thought then. "Birdshit, on my head." And then I thought a whole bunch of other, less genteel thoughts, and started rummaging in my bag for some tissue. But when I got to the top of the stairs, I saw that the building was all roped off for window cleaning, and there were some guys dangling from scaffolding a few floors up, and the white splattery stuff was not birdshit but rather just some sort of industrial window-cleaning product. Not that it's so great to have a drop of industrial window-cleaning product on my head, but I'll take it over birdshit. Any day. (Such a small pleasure, not to be shat upon.)

━ *December 21*

Confession: I have just eaten most of a bag of organic Cheez Doodles. And so what about the "organic" part, especially when that word is immediately followed by "Cheez Doodles." Hooray, somewhat lower in fat; hooray, no genetically modified ingredients; hooray, organic corn, etc. But still. Cheez Doodles. There's no honor in eating a bushel of Cheez Doodles, even faux-hippie Cheez Doodles. All the manuscripts I handle today will be stained orange, and my lips/mouth/tongue feel kind of tender and strange from the influx of salt and sharp corn edges. Oh, and of course while I was deep in a trance, reading work-related material and chomping on said organic Cheez Doodles, the primitive lizard part of my brain apparently decided that my own sock would be a fabulous place to wipe my dusty orange hand. Thus I get the Spaz Award, for that and for the following reason: immediately after the Cheez-Sock Affair I tripped over nothing while carrying a full cup of hot tea and did a spectacular clumsy pirouette and near-total-wipeout, spilling scalding Earl Grey all over my boots and the hem of my skirt. So the entire lower quarter of my body is stained, sullied, and besmirched. *Cleanup on aisle me!*

Last night we went to this "cabaret" thing to see a jazz trio, since two of our friends were involved (bass and piano). It was good, but I feel that I was not adequately forewarned that it would be an entire show of Christmas songs. I could have done without that. When the holiday sentiment got to be too much, I played a little drinking game with myself wherein I took a sip of my cosmopolitan every time the words "Christmas" or "Yule" were sung. That helped a little.

← *December 22*

I had to go to a meeting today with a company bigwig (so different from the rest of us punywigs) who had to give some bad financial news and hand down some unpopular cost-saving edicts, etc. And I was really getting tense and irritable during the meeting because of this man's rhetorical style, which was to seize on one colorful metaphor and return to it periodically. This particular bigwig was fond of saying, "We're not out of the woods yet" and "We've got a flashlight, and we're trying to make a path out of the woods" and other woods-related imagery like that. The problem with colorful metaphors in public speaking is that, to my mind, the speakers never take the colorful metaphors far enough. Why not mention the wolves that no doubt lurk in the woods? Or the fact that the reason we are having trouble making it out of the woods is that we ate fifteen hits of acid and now we are much more interested in rolling around naked in leaf mulch and listening to the stories that trees tell? Why not talk about the member of our woods-traveling party who fell in the creek and now he won't stop bitching about his wet socks and boots and somebody seriously is going to smack him in the mouth unless he shapes up? What about the poison ivy in a rather, ahem, personal area? Or how we're stumbling around with our metaphorical flashlight, metaphorically trying to make it out of the metaphorical woods, and we stumble upon the metaphorical decomposing torso of an alcoholic drifter from Alabama?

TWO BAD THINGS ABOUT CHRISTMAS

1. That Paul McCartney "simply having a wonderful Christmas time" song makes me want to pluck out my eyeballs and hand them to the nearest temporary holiday salesgirl.

2. Every yahoo from god knows where comes downtown to shop. So the streets are full of armies of lost and bewildered suburban women loaded down with shopping bags. They are ruthless, they don't know where they're going exactly, and they have a tendency to just stop dead in the middle of the sidewalk and confer. I was walking down Wabash yesterday lunchtime and one of them yelled to me: "Hey! Is there anything that way?" pointing north. I was confused. "Well . . . civilization doesn't end past Erie Street, if that's what you mean."

← *December 26*

My holiday bender continues apace. I'm on a strict diet of martinis and Christmas cookies (doctor's orders) until the new year. Kicked things off last Friday with Tom at Delilah's, with a lot of beer and a jabbermouth good time. As much as I despise the phrase "the next level," I think that's where our e-mail and link-a-riffic friendship has gone: i.e., I've ceased to worry that he will find me strange during our face-to-face meetings and just settled into being strange.

Some very thoughtful person at work gave me a reprint of an 1827 handbook for butlers, which contains subject headings like "A Most Delicious Salad Sauce." I don't think you can possibly understand how delighted I am by the phrase "A Most Delicious Salad Sauce." Another wonderful gift was from LT, who gave me a garbage disposal (¾ horsepower!), an unheard-of luxury in a 1926-built condominium like ours. I like how LT subverted the rule about not giving your wife appliances for major holidays by giving me a really bad-ass and unglamorous appliance for the holidays. He's a sly postmodern husband, that one. Anyway, since installation will involve both plumbing *and* electricity, we'll have to wait until the new year and get some professionals for the job, as flopping around being electrocuted in three feet of water is no way to spend a holiday.

I gave good presents too, and spent a good chunk of Christmas Eve on a relative's living room floor (relatively sober, honest) helping my cousin put together a LEGO dinosaur. That LEGO dinosaur turned out to be in a ferocious mood and disrupted several board games by trying to devour the pieces. Hey, what can you do.

December 30

GIRL OVERBOARD

I walked across the Michigan Avenue bridge today and noticed how strangely low the railing is, and how one could very easily just hop right over it and jump in the Chicago River. Now, I know that wouldn't be a good idea, and I don't have any particular urge to die by drowning, a broken neck at impact, and/or having my skin peel off from all the pollution. But I *could* jump over, and I wish the railing were higher so that would not be an option.

Similarly, when I used to drive, I would think: how do I know that I won't just suddenly jerk the wheel to the left and go head-on into oncoming highway traffic? I don't think I want to do that, but how do I know that I won't have a strange momentary impulse and do it anyway? Hey, I do stupid shit all the time. Worrying that I _might_ do that led to obsessive, repetitive thoughts that I _would_ do that, sort of without my brain's consent if you will, and led to even less of a desire to drive.

⟵ _January 3_

I have issues with certain types of writing. Particularly well-written, "poignant" essays or memoirs. It seems that writers are always coming to some not-too-dangerous con- clusion while gazing out the window at an ice-bound apple tree or a singing sparrow, and it's just too easy, too perfect, too _Bridges of Madison County_, to be believed. Or they are holding the hand of their dying fathers and realizing what is really important about life. I am not saying that you can't write about holding the hand of your dying father and re- alizing what is really important about life. However, these soft-focus, touchingly well-intentioned (and sometimes even well-written) memoirs never seem to admit any com- plexity in the moment, and they are unabashedly sincere and meaningful in a way I just can't get behind. Do these people not have internal self-observing hypercritical narra- tors or do they simply silence them in order to have their memoir-worthy moments? These writers are selling pro- fundity and I refuse to buy, and I can't tell if that's my fault for being too cranky, theirs for being too predictable, or so- ciety's for swallowing ersatz profundity until we don't have any critical standards and need to be told how to feel.

January 6

THE ASS OF AN INTERLOPER

Every day when I come into work I sit down in my chair and start doing things. Every day, after a while, I notice my chair is adjusted differently. Mostly it's been made taller, and is no longer comfortable for me. I have an office, with a door, but I don't ever lock the door because (a) that doesn't seem to be the culture around here, (b) if I were to walk out the door and get hit by a bus (or, less dramatically, if I were to just call in sick suddenly) other people need to get to my stuff quickly, and (c) I don't have the key, and I'm too lazy to call building services and fill out the several dozen forms that are no doubt required to obtain one. I checked my security logs and it doesn't look like anyone is using my computer (and they wouldn't know my password in any case), and nothing else in my office seems disturbed except the chair, so either it's a member of the cleaning staff taking a break, a coworker who appreciates the peace and quiet that an office with a door can bring, or (the creepiest and least likely possibility) someone who likes to pretend they are me after hours. On Friday I left a note on the chair that said, "Do you use this chair at night? Why?" because I am curious about who's been using the chair, and what their probably nonnefarious purpose is in doing so, but today the note had not been moved and the chair had not been adjusted differently. Maybe I scared the Secret Chair User away. What will really freak me out is if next my instant oatmeal disappears from my bottom drawer, because oatmeal is in a sense a type of porridge, and that combined with the chair makes this whole episode some sort of Goldilocks allegory, with yours truly in an ursine role.

⌐ *January 7*

THE CRANKY

Why? Why is there the cranky? Because it is winter? Because work is trying to kill me? This morning I decided I was really losing it because as I got off the train with all the other worker moles this guy knocked into me from behind and moaned, "God, everyone walks so *slow*" in this irritating queeny voice. (a) I do not walk slow. (b) Even if I were walking slow, this does not give you the right to bump into me more or less on purpose and act like it's nothing. I am used to the urban jostle. Really. I take crowded public transportation every day of my life. This was more like a deliberate push to get me to walk up the stairs at his preferred rate of speed.

Well, whatever, right? Shrug it off, right? Wrong. Because of my generally bad mood lately I got all pissed off about it. For real. The guy had gotten ahead of me, but then became jammed up on the stairs, so as I walked by him I casually let the bag of stuff I was carrying swing jauntily so it hit him in the leg a tiny bit. And then I felt better.

But *shit*. Do I want to be this person? This person who is all subway-rageful for no reason? This person who finds herself stabbing at the Close Door button on the elevator, and, on one particularly bad rageful day, trying to use brain waves to make the doors close faster? The person who came perilously close today at work to saying, *God why can't you people solve your own damn problems for once* when some perfectly nice person came to inform her about another publishing crisis?

I don't. Want to be that person. Help me calm down.

THE NICE

I left work somewhat early and then walked to the south end of downtown to meet LT, who was having a client meeting rather than working at home. Even though the small sharp snow was all small and sharp in my face, and even though I walked almost a mile because I cannot just stand around and wait for the bus, it was nice.

Here are some things I saw on my walk: An empty carton of goat milk. Lots of people not dressed appropriately for the weather. A pizza place that serves a "jumbo slice" + soda for three dollars, an unheard-of bargain downtown and almost worth walking to even from my office, since we have no cheap pizza anywhere around us. A wild-eyed guy in a pith helmet (really!) who asked me directions to Greektown. A bar near the Board of Trade called Stocks and Blondes. (Arrgggggh. Arrgggggh on more than one level, even.) And then LT, leaving his client and meeting me outside, and we walked to Union Station together, and took the Metra train back home. The commuter train is very different from the El. People talk more, and they have shopping bags and luggage and stuff.

We had an errand to run too, which was part of the impetus for leaving work early. LT needs new glasses frames and since we are both kind of blind (me much worse than him . . . if you tried on my glasses you would be able to see forward in time), he needs to bring someone along to tell him how frames look. For being kind of a drab black sweater black jeans guy, he sure has some outré ideas about eyewear. He kept putting on strangely shaped and strangely colored frames until I convinced him that he was no Elvis Costello and no Karl Lagerfeld either.

On the way home we invented a new nonlethal weapon: the tarantula gun. It shoots tarantulas at you. Lots of them. One after the other. Even if you are not afraid of giant hairy spiders, no one wants tarantula goo all over them. We abandoned the idea after realizing that PETA would get all over our asses, but that led right to another idea about a gun that shoots really cute puppies at you, because nothing is bound to depress an enemy so much as a barrage of cute dead puppies, and then we really had to stop talking because we always take everything too far. Besides, it was dinnertime.

◄── *January 8*

I went to a place on our street last night to get some passport pictures taken, because (a) my passport will expire soon, and (b) I am writing a freelance article for this magazine thingy (nothing you have ever heard of), and they demanded a headshot to go with it. I refused. They insisted. I told them to go cram it, Mimi Smartypants does not allow pictures of herself to be published. They showed up at my house and burned me with cigarettes for six hours. I said okay fine you'll get your stinking picture. I thought about giving them a picture of somebody other than me, but that got ruined after the cigarette-burning marathon, since obviously now they know what my face looks like (albeit in a contorted and sweaty way). So off to the photo place I trudged, and I sat on a small stool and made an attempt to smile, but you know what? No. I will use these photographs for the updated passport, because I don't really care what customs officials think, but for a publication, even one that will only be distributed to certain carefully selected geeks, I would rather have a photograph that doesn't make me look like a subterranean creature from a lousy fantasy novel. (However, I wouldn't mind having one that made me look like a big-breasted cartoon warrior queen, with a sword and shield, riding on a flying unicorn, also from a lousy fantasy novel. What I really should do is just submit a picture of She-Ra, Princess of Power.) The photographer sat me down on a too-low stool so my head is just sort of peeking up into the frame, and since it was the end of the day my hair had decided to say a big *Fuck you* to the effort I had put into making it unwavy, and my glasses did something weird in the photo so that it looks like I have big dark circles under my eyes. Or maybe I really do have big dark circles under my eyes. And my facial expression in the photos is almost a Johnny Rotten–esque curled-lip sneer, and that's not good because people will sit down (or stand up, or recline in the bath, or kneel in between dry heaves, heck, I don't care) to read my article and take one look at the photo and say, "Oh yeah? You think you're better than me, you Little Sneering Freakish Sleep-Deprived Elf? Think again!" and cancel their subscriptions. So the passport photos for the headshot article are a no-go. Maybe

I can get LT to take pictures of my head with the digital camera this weekend.

←—*January 9*

I have a problem where I just don't feel a hundred percent, and it's nothing easily identifiable like a sore throat or a stomachache, and let's just get this out of the way right now: I know it's probably nothing. I mean, I can joke about how I am positive I have The Cancer, but I don't want you to think that I really am one of those freaky people who is this close to starting a regimen of daily shark-blood injections, or taking out a second mortgage in order to be able to afford one of those full-body scans, or whatever. I do not feel entirely right, and maybe what I should do is readjust my conception of what it means to feel good to this new, lower standard, and then I would be able to say, "I feel great!" and be truthful about it. I have also given up worrying about whether this not-feeling-so-fantastic is a body thing or a mind thing, because I am sure the answer is "both." And that way lies madness. And this way sits madness. And over this way loiters madness, leaning against the wall, smoking a cigarette. Lazy madness, get a fucking job.

THE SYMPTOMS OF MY MYSTERY ILLNESS

1. Sometimes I feel like my skeleton is trying to get out of my body and dance around in a grotesque macabre fashion while the rest of me slumps to the floor like a wet bag of cat food.

2. Nothing tastes particularly good to me.

3. I have a near-constant stuffed-up nose, which should not be happening now that all the leaves are gone.

4. I am a big whiner, and am going to stop this now.

◄─ *January 10*

IN WHICH I AM THE VICTIM OF A CLUMSY SEDUCTION ATTEMPT BY A POLISH CONTRACTOR

Last week I had to go to a work-related party, and of course I left too early and got to the Andersonville neighborhood too early. Who wants to be early to a party? Making small talk while the hostess runs around filling chip bowls and such? So I stopped at a local bar for some preparty holiday cheer, and I loaded up the jukebox with ten or fifteen Jesus and Mary Chain and Mercury Rev songs, much to the probable chagrin of the few old men who were at the bar, but too bad. That first beer was quite enjoyable, and really, who wants to be "on time" for a party? So I had another. As I was finishing that, the pile of tan work jacket on the stool next to mine suddenly shifted around and started to make noise. "Whoa," it said. "Whoa whoa whoa whoa whoa." This did not seem to require comment, so I finished my beer and stood up to put on my coat. The movement seemed to further animate the tan work jacket pile, and it lifted its head to resolve into a more human shape, pitching forward alarmingly on its stool and increasing in volume: "*Whoa*! You are a *stone fox*!"

This did not deter me from continuing with the coat and

leaving process, but it did make me laugh. I mean, when was the last time you were called a "stone fox"? If you are me the answer is "never."

"Siddown siddown siddown," Mr. Jacket slurred at me. "My name's Bob. Let me buy you a drink." He made no actual move to buy me a drink (which was fine because I really *had to leave*), but he kept talking anyway, and I learned these things:

1. Bob is Polish and a contractor, and you want to know who runs this city? Polish contractors.

2. Bob has been drinking since 1 P.M. and I can't tell at all, can I? Can I? Tell Bob the truth.

3. Bob has Iraqis on his crew and it's too bad we are going to blow their country up because they are damn fine workers.

This was all very compelling but I needed to go to my party, so I continued with the coat and bag-gathering process, and suddenly Bob's mood turned serious and confessional. He leaned in all Scotch-breath close, I suddenly noticed the gold coke spoon glinting among a thicket of gray chest hair, and it began to dawn on me that I may be dealing with a Major League Freak. "Aw, don't leave," said Bob. "You are such a fox! You are the kind of girl I could say things to. Things like *strap-on, watersports, girl-on-girl*. Things like *nipple clamps*. Am I right or am I right? Here, call me if you want to play, and bring your boyfriend, I'm bi." Now I was the one thinking, Whoa whoa whoa whoa whoa, as he scribbled his phone number on a napkin, and I accepted it because I was really too dazed to do anything else.

This scenario raises a few questions.

1. First, is there something about me that is particularly attractive to middle-aged Polish contractors?

2. "You are the kind of girl I could say things to." What the hell is that supposed to mean? Do I give off a kinky aura? Or is he just prepared to get a lot of drinks thrown in his face until he finds the right girl?

3. And finally, why didn't I just shut him down? I am not shy about that sort of thing: I have a great icy stare and a bad case of sass-mouth. But for some reason this freak started reciting the *Penthouse* letters page at me and I just let him do it. Maybe I'm addicted to novelty, in the form of dirty-talking strangers in bars.

Anyway, I did throw his phone number away, so I'm not *that* desperate for new experiences, thank you very much.

⟵ *January 12*

I got a belated birthday present from my father-in-law and his wife. And it is quite an amazing thing. Not amazing as in "Wow, that was an amazing dinner." More like amazing as in "Holy shit! That giant wart on your face is amazing!"

I now own a Polarfleece poncho. If your mind reels (as mine did), break it down into its component parts. Polarfleece. Poncho. First of all, who wears ponchos? Why would anyone except the severely mentally ill cut a hole in a blanket and think, "This is now a garment?" (Note: if you are a gaucho, or a Mexican person in some 1950s racist cartoon, I will cut you some slack on the poncho front.)

Also: Polarfleece. I have nothing against Polarfleece per se. I think it makes a lovely, if somewhat synthetic, blanket or pullover. But a Polarfleece poncho is *a lot* of Polarfleece. Also, the poncho, in its mistaken "one size fits all" philosophy, is huge on me. LT made me try it on and then couldn't stop laughing. It comes down to my ankles. It is a sort of floor-length Polarfleece evening gown. (Perfect for those winter formals!)

So that's in the bag of giveaways that hopefully we will get around to donating to the thrift store this weekend. Hey, one woman's Polarfleece poncho is another woman's great thrifting find. I think.

I feel a bit guilty about ridiculing this gift here. Am I just an ungrateful person? I mean, I was very polite and everything when I opened it. Ah, screw it. I think even Oprah and her freaking gratitude journal would have a hard time feeling thankful for a Polarfleece poncho.

⟵ *January 13*

Last night LT was at the gym, lifting weights, and I was at home on the couch using my own underdeveloped muscles to lift my book. No music was playing, but the stereo was on, because I never remember to turn it off. I was lying there reading and I heard a loud male voice, which sounded like it was inside my house, say

"Okay, I will just bring it around here. Heading up Devon Avenue now."

I froze, and freaked, and wondered if I imagined it, and then thought: Oh, maybe it is someone talking on the intercom. Then a different male voice said, "Ten-four," and why would you say, "Ten-four" on an apartment intercom? Just buzz the guy in, don't play Starsky to his Hutch. The freaking intensified. The voices kept talking among themselves. My second thought: Hmm, maybe this is it, and—instead of God speaking to me, or an evil demon whispering, "Go after the mayor's eyes with a melon ball scooper"—maybe this is the prosaic and utterly irritating way I will go crazy: hearing phantom cabbies trade locations and bid for rides. When LT came home he explained to me how any piece of wire can become an antenna, and that is why nearby cabbies' voices were being relayed through my stereo. I guess my sanity is intact for the time being.

◄—*January 16*

Last night was a total wash. I was sad and cranky when I got home, and almost felt like I was coming down with something, so frowny was my mouth and so achy were my joints. I made an effort for a little while, screwing around online and eating leftover pizza (and I learned something: two minutes is too long in the microwave for one piece of pizza. The cheese was *boiling*.) Around 8:30, however, I couldn't take it anymore and crawled into bed, emergency shutdown mode, before my thoughts could get any darker or before I could break out the wine and start writing juvenile pitiful prose or stream-of-consciousness e-mails to baffled friends. Or worse.

When I was about to microwave the pizza I noticed that there are *microwave instructions* printed on the inside of the microwave door. I never noticed them before. So I was reading the inside of the microwave door, which tells you how you can microwave based on a food ("object") paradigm rather than a time-based or how-hot-you-want-it ("subject") paradigm. There were all these "codes" listed (press 1 for coffee, 2 for reheated pasta, etc.). Also, my microwave has a "child lock" feature that I never knew about. Apparently I can lock children into my microwave oven. Or wait, probably it is used to lock children *out* of my microwave oven. I find this a bit useless. If I cannot trust my hypothetical child not to microwave the cat, even though I have clearly instructed him or her not to microwave the cat, perhaps I have bigger problems that cannot be solved through technology. And any kid who is so devious as to continue with the quest to microwave the cat, despite my edicts and despite my child lockingness, can probably climb up on a chair and read the instructions on how to disable the child lock.

◄── *January 17*

I really love the newly discovered (by me) text-messaging capability of my cell phone. It is pleasant to be on the bus and get a little "hello" from someone. It solves the twin problems of how (1) I often have trouble hearing my phone ring what with all the city noise around me, and (2) that when the phone does ring in a quiet place it startles me nearly into catalepsy. It also solves the social anxiety problem of wanting to communicate with someone but not wanting to do something as boorish and intrusive as making their phone ring. And it is good for those non-emergency drinking sessions, not so much *Help I am stranded here surrounded by idiots but drinks are half-price get here now,* but rather *I seem to have found myself at a bar near your house come by if you are not busy.* LT has discovered that he can text-message me from the cell phone company's website, and enjoys doing this whenever he needs a little break from programming, with the result being that I often get strange messages like *Urgent call back immediately my scrotum is wrinkled!!!!*

← *January 20*

MY UNBELIEVABLY EMBARRASSING AND SITCOM-ESQUE MOMENT

Okay. Yesterday I got my hand stuck in a vending machine. Only me, folks, only me. And I wasn't trying to steal anything. I had skipped breakfast and by 11 A.M. was absolutely going to starve to death, so I headed down to the vending machines on the second floor for some Wheat Thins. Man, do I love Wheat Thins.

The door on this particular vending machine is somewhat broken, although I didn't know it at the time. The springs have given out so that one must push astoundingly hard, with both hands, in order to get the door to open more than just a tiny bit. The tiny bit that the door does open is not large enough to reach into and get your snack.

Unless you're me and have tiny little hands. I didn't even notice that the opening was smaller than usual, I just reached right in. And got my hand stuck. I have kind of a big clunky watch, and the face of it was too tall to get my hand out. I couldn't even rotate my hand. Yikes.

So I was kneeling down and with my other hand trying to reach in there and get the clasp of my watch undone, thinking that if it will come off I could back my hand out. It was way past the coffee rush hour, so there was no one around. I was trying to be cool, but also starting to panic a little bit, because my hand was *really really* stuck.

A woman walked by and didn't notice me struggling. After five more minutes I was still trapped when a guy walked by, so I gave in to my own essential dorkitude and said, "Um, help? I'm stuck?"

To his credit, he didn't laugh or anything. In fact, he took my plight very seriously, like a *Rescue 911* situation or something, going, "Oh my god" and dropping down beside me to help with the extraction. I was finally able to get the watch undone, rotate my bruised and red hand, and pull it out.

I made him go back in the vending machine to get my watch and my snack. No way was I sticking my hand in there again.

What a geek I am. Do you think I could write this harrowing tale up for *Reader's Digest*? Or maybe one of those newsmagazine "Survivor's Stories"?

⟵ *January 23*

There is something about Chicago I'll bet anything you didn't know. It's not in any guidebook. And that is the fact that Chicago's citizens feel compelled to show me their genitalia on public transportation. It's true, and it has happened to me multiple times. They ride the train, they see me board, and they reach into their collective pants.

Once, I was riding the El train rather late at night, minding my own business, when I noticed the guy across from me fiddling around inside his sweatpants. Okay, I think, he's just adjusting. God knows we all need to do some adjusting from time to time. Go back to my book. The next time I look up the adjusting has changed to pumping, stroking, whatever you want to call it. He was very definitely, obviously, pleasuring himself. And he wasn't doing it *at* me (in fact, his eyes are closed), but in my field of vision nonetheless, and it is not acceptable. The El is public space, people. Have some regard for the social contract.

I looked around the rest of the car, and it was obvious to me that other people have noticed, but they were ignoring the Masturbating Man as hard as they can; noses buried in papers etc. Meanwhile, he was still going at it.

I tried giving him my best evil look, but if anything that just inspires the guy. Finally I couldn't take it anymore, so I stood up and announced to the entire car, "Ladies and gentlemen, this man is masturbating. Let's all give him a round of applause!" and start clapping.

Some people laughed, some people clapped with me, and of course the majority just thought, "Oh god look at the crazy lady," but I felt better that something was said. And the guy was sufficiently embarrassed to get off (no, not like that) at the next stop.

⟵ *January 27*

When I was a child, my mother never cut my sandwich into triangles. I don't know why, but it was always rectangles. The only time I ever saw a triangle sandwich was in a restaurant, and in my head I still think of this sort of sandwich cut as "fancy." LT made me a grilled cheese and cut it into triangles, and I went, "Oooh! Just like at the diner!" and explained my sandwich history to him, and he thought it was kind of sad. No, it is not abuse or neglect or satanic rituals, but it is deprivation of a sort and should be enough for me to write a depressing memoir about my childhood and get on a daytime talk show.

⟵ *January 31*

Most of the time I just feel like myself, but sometimes I like to pretend to bitch and moan about how I feel old. I like to tell my sister (who's younger) tales like this: I remember making popcorn *on the stove*. I remember having a *rotary-dial phone* and that the area code, even in the suburbs, was 312. I remember *buying tapes* and thinking that Screeching Weasel was a good band. I remember wearing petticoats and combat boots and thrift store tuxedo jackets and fingerless gloves and black lipstick, all at the same time.

My sister is very good at faking being impressed.

⟵ *February 3*

I tend to get minor respiratory viruses and things a lot, and some sort of serious bronchial infection once a year or so. But you know what I am kind of weirdly proud of? I never throw up. I have not thrown up in about fifteen years. I have traveled to the Third World, drunk tequila until last call, smoked Egyptian cigarettes on a bumpy, smelly bus, and I still don't get sick.

My theory (one of them: oh how many theories I have! if you only knew) is that the world is divided into Pukers and Nonpukers. My sister-in-law throws up during pretty much every hangover she has. Kat throws up if she eats shellfish or too much dairy. Come to think of it, Kat throws up if you even look at her funny. Okay, I exaggerate, but she is firmly in the first category. Now before you get all riled up, please note that I am not saying the Nonpukers are *better* than the Pukers or anything like that. If anything, the Pukers may even have a slight advantage over us Nonpukers, as they are able to take vomiting in stride, and be all blasé about it, whereas for me vomiting would be very traumatic and I would probably freak out and cry and eat only bland plain rice for a week out of fear. So no matter what your puking category, be proud.

⟵ *February 9*

Here's how I normally behave at a party. I drink cocktails. I try to talk to everyone who seems interesting. I tell funny stories. (At least I think they're funny.) I eat snack food. I may even dance a little, in a muted and subdued way, if it is that sort of party. What I do not do is pick a fight with total strangers. That's why my Friday night experience was so very odd, as a young man insisted on engaging me in conversation and then being contrary and illogical and more or less trying to provoke me. He attempted to argue with me about film and theater and meaningful work for a while, which I mostly just shrugged off, but his mission in life to disagree with me about absolutely everything quickly became absurd. At one point I made some light-hearted joke about fucking a goat (because nothing gets laughs like bestiality, folks), and this person immediately got on my case about how dare I insinuate that sex with a goat is not real sex, and let's define our terms, and I am obviously a prude for not being cool and hip and open enough to admit that fucking a goat can ever be construed as a Good Thing. At that point I just had to walk away laughing. Tonight on *Face the Nation*, a roundtable discussion about the merits of goat buggery.

Saturday night was much better and less combative, tapas and lots of sangria, and snuggling with my very gay and very snuggly friend Dan. He's just so damn snuggly. I think he may be partially composed of fabric softener.

← *February 10*

The very best thing happened to me just now. I was on the bus going home, and it was insanely crowded, and what's the best thing to go along with "insanely crowded"? An insane person! Yes! There seriously has to be some way we can get the mentally ill to ride public transit at only off-peak hours. Maybe I will write to the mayor about that. Anyway, this particular insane person was an old lady with some sort of religious psychosis, ranting about Jesus, etc., and here are some quotes free of charge: "I walk with the Holy Ghost" (I'm sure you do), "America is an evil country" (okay, that's debatable, but at least you can live your full insane life in relative freedom and peace here), and "The Jews reject God. Soon the world will go to war against the Jews" (given the bus route you're on, you may want to lay off comments of that nature. We know you are just a crazy old lady but some of these Lubavitchers are pretty burly and sensitive). Oh, and of course she had that whole echolalia thing going on and thus, like some demented preacher (which in a sense she was), had to say each of her crazy statements at least three times, at top volume. Normally I am very tolerant of the bus-riding crazies, but I felt tired and cranky on this particular day, so when she launched into a hideously misinformed anti-choice rap: "We got mothers killing their own children. Not even animals do that!" I just had to come out with, "Oh sure they do. Haven't you ever had a hamster?"

This got some stifled laughter from the rest of the bus (thank you, thank you very much. I'll be here all week), but it did not deter her. It did, however, have an unexpected but welcome side effect: her eyes got real wide and she yelled, *"Are you Satan?"* to which I could only nod and grin wildly and flash her the devil-horns hand sign, Motley Crüe–style (well, what would you have done?). She freaked and shuffled away from me muttering "I can't stand next to Satan. Oh no, I can't stand next to Satan. Oh help me Jesus," etc. I suppose I should feel bad taking advantage of some unfortunate woman's particular psychosis, but if it buys me some breathing room and peace and quiet on the commute home, that's fine with me.

⟵ *February 13*

VARATIONS ON A STUPID THEME

1. Tickle Me Elmo
2. Sue Me Snoopy
3. Garrote Me Gonzo
4. Borrow My Bartok CD and Forget to Give It Back Barney
5. Bitchslap Me Bert
6. Grope Me Grover
7. Ostracize Me Oscar

⟵ *February 14*

Someone on the other side of my office has decorated her cubicle with the freakiest Valentine's Day decorations, they are freaking me the freak out and I want you to come over here, hold my hand, and feed me Valium until I feel normal again. This woman's entire cube is covered with these big-headed Precious Moments children, "I Wuv You This Much," and I guess these hydrocephalic monsters are supposed to be in love? Or something. There is one in particular that I cannot deal with, it features the hydrocephalic boy and the hydrocephalic girl facing each other, with a lot of bubbly cartoon hearts, and they are holding a kitten between them. To me it looks like these children are moments away from tearing the kitten apart and stuffing its kitten flesh into their creepily similar pink rosebud mouths. Like they are just about to smear their extraordinarily creepy child-sized wedding clothes with kitten blood. I don't know about you, but hydrocephalic Precious Moments children with moist blank eyes dismembering and eating kittens does not exactly scream *Happy Valentine's Day* to me, and on my way to the fax machine I have to run by this woman's cube with my eyes closed, and let us hope she takes it down promptly when the holiday is over because I do not think I can take it much longer.

February 17

To capitalize on the glut of business books and management seminars that is such a thriving and insipid industry in this country, I would like to work with the ghost of Hunter S. Thompson to develop a management seminar that we can take to hotel ballrooms and corporate training centers across America. Actually, I don't really need his posthumous help, just his name and endorsement. We'll call it "Loathing, Fear, and Effective Leadership" or "It Never Gets Weird Enough When You're CEO" or some other, catchier title. And I will give an inspirational speech on how to do an employee performance evaluation when you are sweating on mescaline, how to handle it when big orange spiders are crawling out of the copier, the stress-relieving benefits of keeping a bottle of Cuervo in your bottom desk drawer, and how to motivate employees by threatening them with large handguns. The seminar will run from 9 A.M. to 11:30 A.M., and then we'll break for "coffee," and then the fluorescent lights will start oscillating and the cubicle walls will close in and melt. Bathrooms are in the back if you need to get away, but please make sure you're back in time for our role-playing game.

⟵ *February 19*

This marks the second night in a row that I have been awakened out of a deep sleep by exquisitely painful leg cramps. At 2:30 this morning I was sitting up in bed trying not to scream or whimper too loudly and wake up LT, flexing my foot and pounding on my knotted-up calf. I read in one of my numerous medical reference books that nighttime leg cramps can be a sign of a mineral deficiency, so if you will excuse me I'm going to go outside and lick some rocks now.

— *February 22*

Only LT and I are crazy enough to go to London in February, but we have friends in the city and the fares were too low to pass up. I have trouble sleeping on planes (ha ha are we surprised? no we are not) but on the way there I was determined to make an effort. LT has much less of a problem than I and he was using the eyeshade (stupidly, we only brought one). I had a large white handkerchief with me so I tied that around my head blindfold-style. I also like to keep my hands together when I sleep (I'm a compact sleeper), and I had my hair out of the ponytail, and the ponytail holder (some of you might call it a *scrunchie* but I despise that term) around one wrist, and at some point during my light doze I must have inserted the other wrist into it as well, like a single fabric handcuff. It was only after I woke up that I realized how strange I must have looked to anyone passing down the aisle, like a miniature hostage crisis or prisoner transport.

On this particular vacation I became a swirling vortex of primal need. I ate *a lot*. I slept *a lot*. I have probably been to London a few too many times to get excited about it in a touristic sense. However, I did visit a few local attractions. The toy museum featured some wonderful creepy dolls and a 1930s construction toy (a sort of proto-LEGO) named Ubuilda (as in Ubuilda Bridge, Ubuilda Fort, Ubuilda Castle). It totally put me in mind of some Sicilian ancestor of mine waving his arms above his head and shouting "Ubuilda bridge, goddammit! Whattsa matta you?" I also spent a day in Greenwich, looking at the Thames and climbing around on the *Cutty Sark* and visiting the National Maritime Museum. LT and I almost got thrown out of there for asking where the interactive Bugger the Cabin Boy exhibit could be found, but can you blame us? How can you expect to talk about nineteenth-century maritime pursuits without mentioning drunkenness and sodomy? (Come to think of it, how do we manage to talk about anything without mentioning drunkenness and sodomy? Those topics keep coming up no matter what you do. Or maybe that's just me.)

◂── *February 25*

You already know that sleep and me have a bit of a strained relationship. But there is more pathology than meets the eye. I also have a huge problem with Slumber Party Syndrome, which means this: (1) I will be tired and yawny and LT will say, "Let's go to bed," and we will. (2) The minute the lights go out I am wide awake. I am, in fact, all hepped up and goofy and giggly. I suddenly have all kinds of things I want to tell LT. He is a patient man, but he is also the sort of man who (quite reasonably) wants to *sleep* when he goes to bed, so he will ask me, "Uh, I thought we were going to sleep now?" and I will apologize and settle down briefly before starting to chuckle in the dark again at something I thought in my little brain. Last night took the cake, though. I had this movie idea. (I won't get into it now except that it involved Monkey Man, that anecdotal creature that was terrorizing India a few years back. If the film industry does not capitalize on Monkey Man they are dumber than I ever thought. It would be especially cool if the Hindi film industry made a movie with Monkey Man, and he sang and danced, and a beautiful coquettish woman in a sari danced with him in the rain, with her sari all wet and clingy, and then she fell in love with him, realizing he's not so ugly after all, and Monkey Man turns out to be some sort of Robin Hood–ish freedom fighter, and at one point receives a minor but dashing head wound and has to tie a strip of cloth around his Monkey Man head, Rambo-style. But I digress.) Anyway, I was explaining my movie idea to LT in the dark, only in much greater detail and in a much more exciting fashion, and I realize he hasn't made any noise in a while, and he's asleep. But five minutes later he rolled over and we had this exchange:

LT: Oh wow, I just dozed off and dreamed about Monkey Man.

Me: *No you quesadilla-head, that was my movie that I just told you about.*

LT [asleep again]: . . .

← *February 28*

Recently, suddenly, there were ants in my back bathroom. There was something wrong with these tiny black ants. I think these ants were a little bit retarded. LT is a messy cook, and there are often crumbs on the kitchen floor, yet the ants never ventured out there but stayed in the back bathroom, where there is no food. My bathroom ants rode the short bus. My bathroom ants wore hockey equipment and they weren't even on a team. LT bought some ant traps and the ants totally fell for it, and now there are dead ants in the bathroom that need sweeping up (I know, I know, I'll get to it), but there are no more living ants. It was almost pathetically easy to wipe them out, and my respect for the insect kingdom has slipped a notch.

⟵ *March 3*

I had an idea for a video game. I am just a fountain of ideas lately. Here's my idea: there are plenty of video games that allow you to shoot zombies or drive racecars or build entire civilizations all on your lonesome. But, as far as I know, there are no video games that let you work on a banana boat all day. Loading bananas, watching out for the deadly black tarantula, avoiding the cruel overseer, waiting for the tallyman to show his lazy ass. Daylight comes and you want to go home. You (virtually) stack bananas until the morning comes. We already have the theme music, now we just need graphics and programming, this is going to be awesome, all the kids will be loading virtual bananas onto virtual banana boats, six foot seven foot eight foot *bunch*, and totally neglecting their homework. *Heed my words Nintendo executives*. Heed them.

⟵ *March 4*

I wish so much of my thoughts weren't all tangled up with my moods. I either want to (a) live up to my self-conception of being a logical and thoughtful person, all the time, and not let minor things like Crushing Despair with No Root Cause enter my world, or (b) become a creature solely of mood, and let my overdeveloped self-awareness muscles atrophy. Because when I am being stupid, as above, I know that I am being stupid, and when I am happy I think, "Is this me, being happy? Is this what happiness is for me?" and when I am depressed I am never able to fully give in to it, because I totally recognize every little symptom for what it is, and I get all strict and disciplinarian and call myself on my bullshit, and I become irritated with my stupid overdramatic neurochemical system, and I end up just wanting to get over myself already. Which does nothing to fix the depression, but which does add another lovely little layer of self-loathing on top of everything.

You know what, though? I have made a decision to stop obsessing about the fact that there is something wrong with me and accept my baseline bleak outlook as just another genetic or environmentally developed trait. Love me, love my bleak. This is known as the Fuck It Philosophy, and although it does not usually make an appearance until Friday evening, there is nothing I need more right now than a nice big syrupy tablespoon of Fuck It, and I suspect you could use some too. Open wide.

← *March 6*

Want to hear something gross? I think that you do. Okay. I have not changed my sheets in quite a while. In fact, I do not have a clear memory in my mind of the most recent sheet-changing jamboree. (Changing the sheets does not deserve to be called a jamboree, but I really wanted to use the word "jamboree" at least once today, and now! That goal! Has been! Accomplished! I! Rule!)

I rule, that is, except when it comes to changing the sheets regularly and not being a vile disgusting little girl with dirty sheets. I have not had the energy to change the damn sheets, and I think that makes me a loser instead.

Until today. I got up early, showered (see, I am not *that* gross), dressed, and got picked up by my paintergrrrl friend for breakfast at Earwax. Which lasted around four hours, because the hippie waiter guy (who definitely had not been as conscientious as I about that whole shower-ing/clean clothes thing) kept coming around with the cof-fee, and it is hard for me to say no to beverages. So after four hours of caffeine and sharing silly anecdotes, with the occasional break for somewhat serious discussion about the bizarre process of being Taught to Make Art, she left to do useful things (like maybe changing her sheets) and I stayed there, drinking more caffeine and getting more strange. My spine felt like a glass harmonica and at one point I felt scared of my own coat. When your coat scares you, you have had too much caffeine. I typed a lot on my laptop too, because if I don't type at least one thousand words a day, whether it is silly Internet crap like this or more thoughtful private writing, I start to feel like I am losing molecules, losing definition, my edges getting blurry, and I feel like I might just disappear. I am inter-ested in the edges of things and the way they poke and in-trude into their surrounding space. If I were a painter that is what I would paint. I am not a painter so instead I just type lots and lots of words in an effort to stay three-dimensional and not go curling up at the edges like an old stamp or blowing away in the wind like a leaf.

What was my point? Did I have a point? Oh point, where are you? I can hear the point crying off in the distance, very faintly, like a neglected child left to lie in its crib all day. The point is crying out for its bottle and I am the point's irresponsible junkie mother, on the nod with the needle still in my arm, and the point's cries register only dimly, and here comes Point Protective Services to place the point with a foster family.

Ah. The point is that I changed the sheets. The Change the Sheets Imperative came over me all at once when I got home from the café. "This is it," I thought. "These sheets must be changed. Before any more manly, husbandly seed is spilled, before any more drool is drooled, before any more sick junkie sweat is sweated as I once again try to kick my Gummi worm habit, twisting and writhing in the sheets with visions of wonderfully colorful segmented gelatin trembling before my eyes, *I am going to change these sheets.*"

So I did.

◄— *March 9*

Here's a paradox for you. I love minutiae and I always want to know what people are thinking. However, it is so very wrong to ask somebody, "What are you thinking?" *Never ask this.* When your significant other or best friend gets that faraway look and you ask, "What are you thinking?" you are going to be very disappointed when the answer is "How vile it is to use the word 'nugget' in context of a chicken product" or "Whether I should just go for it and shave off all my pubic hair" or "*The Chicago Manual of Style*'s recommendation on alphabetizing German proper names." Never, ever, ask directly. Instead create an atmosphere of warm loving encouragement wherein people want to tell you what they are thinking, spontaneously and without prompting. Then you can use that atmosphere of warm loving encouragement to tell them how totally, completely nuts they are.

◄— *March 12*

Last night LT went to his evening Chinese class (isn't he such an overachiever?). After I had my bachelorette dinner (which was quite sensible, rather than the Refrigerator Roulette I sometimes indulge in), I had this crazy idea. The idea hit me with that giddy powerful feeling you get from varnishing floors in an unventilated room, and had similar properties in that the idea seemed extremely glittery and attractive and I felt as if I gazed down upon the idea from a great lofty height, and saw that it was good. Here was the idea: *I shall make some muffins.* Where did the idea come from? Well, I did flip through that issue of *Martha Stewart Living* while waiting for my tax guy appointment. And I have always wanted to be the sort of person who can Do Things—you know, like those people who are always running around changing their own tires and making their own stationery and whipping up a batch of muffins for no reason at all, while I stand around flopping my spastic stick arms and saying, "Uh . . . if you need any books read, I can help with that. Or how about drinking this here can of beer? No problem. Glad to be of service."

So I found a muffin recipe and realized I had all the ingredients, including a bag of leftover cranberries in the freezer. Left over from what? I don't know. I buy groceries in a state of blackout sometimes. However, I did not read the recipe very well. It called for one and one-quarter cups of sugar in the ingredient list, and then said "Combine sugar and cranberries over high heat and stir until sugar is dissolved." Are you sure? I thought as I stirred and stirred and stirred a red, grainy, sugary, cranberry-studded mass. Lo and behold (thank you, laws of chemistry), the sugar did, eventually, dissolve. Then I go to read about the dry ingredients and find listed, among the flour, baking powder, etc., "and the remaining quarter-cup sugar." Remaining? Fuck. Improvising, I left it out of the dry stuff and trusted that my over-sugared cranberries would carry the day. Also improvising, I decided there was not any need to let my butter soften *completely*, I mean, it's soft *enough*, right? and so I went ahead with the hand mixing of the butter, eggs, and milk, using the hand mixer which, when running, smells of a serious impending electrical fire but which also was a Gift from My Dead Grandmother, so of course I can't get rid of it. So because the butter had not been adequately softened, the hand mixer whirled butter clots everywhere and large lipomas of butter ended up trapped in the beaters. Improvising even further, I retardedly tried to push the butter globs out of the beaters while the beaters were still moving, with a knife, which made an amazing avant-garde noise-band screeching clattering sound and scared The Cat. The batter, when finally combined with the cranberries, looked horrible and vaguely intraoperative, but by that point my muffin adventure was sort of like America's involvement in the Vietnam War—hideous, prolonged, and starting to feel futile, but with the oven preheated and the protesters marching outside the White House I had no choice but to press on.

Twenty minutes later we had achieved muffinosity and they really are not bad. Kind of architecturally low to the ground, nothing like your Mega McMuffin Mansions sold by Starbucks or anything, but tasty enough. I brought some to work and left them by the fax machine with a sign that said: FREE NONPOISONOUS MUFFINS! BAKED BY MIMI! DON'T BE SCARED!

← *March 17*

I hate Irish bars. Well, if they are just normal Chicago old-man shot-and-a-beer bars that happen to be owned by an Irish-named guy, that's fine, but I hate bars that try to make a point of their Irishness, because I just don't care. LT and I were in the car and thinking of some over-the-top names for fake Irish bars:

Paddy Mac's Shamrock Station
Finnegan's Lake . . . O'Whiskey
O'Paddy McFlanagin's
Darby Upchuck
The Potato Pub

Yer Brother's a Faggot and Yer Sister's a Whore Bar and
 Grill
The Naked Leprechaun

Although I vowed to be a big old hermit on this Weekend of Savage Stupidity, it ended up not working out that
way. (Digression on my own digression, because I just
thought of another reason to hate Saint Patrick's Day: can
you think of another holiday that encourages face painting
to a similar degree? Yuck.) Friday I managed the hermitty
thing just fine. LT worked on coding some web page all
night, so we ordered in Thai and had beer. Even though I
only had *two lousy beers* I think one of them was called
"Date Rape Ale," or maybe the sinus medicine I had taken
earlier did not mesh well with it. Because soon I became
very woozy and rubber-legged and eventually gave up trying to follow the plot of the movie I was halfheartedly
watching, opting instead to lie on the floor listening to
music and periodically yelling at the ceiling to not get any
funny ideas. Don't get smart with me, Ceiling! I'm warning
you! The Cat seemed concerned about my lying on the
floor and kept coming over and poking me in the chest
with her paw, like she was trying to take my pulse, which
I guess is reassuring in case I ever really do keel over or OD.
 Saturday I met up with Tom at Delilah's quite early,
around six, and getting off the El at Diversey even at that
early hour was insane. It was like running a gauntlet of
sweaty green-shirted drunken hooting nitwits, like Tail-
hook without the touching, like something out of Hierony-
mus Bosch, like something that could practically make you
long for the Taliban to take over Lincoln Park and sober it

up a bit. And believe me, I am not an advocate of sobriety—
in fact the first thing I did at Delilah's was bond with the
bartender over the sheer hellish miasma of Saint Patrick's
Day and join him in a shot of tequila, the most un-Irish
liquor we could think of.

← March 20

HAM ALIVE

1. "Ham alive!" would be a good old-timey exclamation.
"Well, ham alive! You done near scared me to death, boy!"

2. Or Ham Alive could be a children's toy. Not a baby doll
but a ham, and not with a mouth exactly, but with a sort
of wet gaping meaty orifice. Ah quit crying kid, you are
lucky you got anything at all for Christmas. Your dad
stayed up all night gouging a mouth-shaped hole into that
canned ham and this is the thanks he gets? Get Mommy
another beer.

3. Ham Alive could also be the code name for an unpleasant genetic engineering proposal to create a sentient
ham. Would you like to see the lab? The prototypes are
fairly grotesque but what can you do. Those Greenpeace
types are going to *wish* we stuck with the hybrid corn and
the fish genes in the tomatoes! Bwahahahahaha! Easter
dinner is going to be pretty weird from now on, with sentient ham!

4. Maybe *Ham Alive!* is the newest Broadway musical!
Singing, dancing, acting hams! A touching tale about a

giant ham, created in a laboratory, who can think and feel! And all he wants is to be loved!

5. Or "ham alive" can just be something you put on the grocery list, for no reason, and it can keep you and your husband in stitches all the way to the store, because you both are very easily amused.

In related news, we also invented the porkulele, which is a ukulele made of pork. We are ridiculous people.

← *March 24*

Do you know how much I hate wedding showers? Do you know how much I hate attending wedding showers while hungover? Because that was my Sunday. I find it very hard to gush and enthuse about towels and bakeware at any time, much less when I have a pounding headache and feel all cold and clammy.

That sounds like a snack item: New Cold N' Clammy!

And why was I hungover? Because, people, you have got to stop giving me free stuff. LT and I went to go see Shelley's band, because it is so much fun to see people you work with every day wear glitter tights and take guitar solos and generally behave like rock stars. I drank some beer, and then it turned out that the cheap draft was free for all the band members, and we just happened to know the band, so they got me some more beer, and then the bartender bought me a beer, and then the bartender bought me a shot of tequila (I think she thought I was cute or something), and before I know it it's last call and I'm drunk. During the entire evening the rational part of my brain is saying, "Okay, that's enough, say no to the next one," but then another free beer would appear (hey, that rhymes! sing it!) and the dark evil lizard part of my brain would make my hand reach for it.

All better now, though. Actually, I probably would have been fine if I had been able to lie in my bed and get over it, but nooooo, I had to go be a girl and enthuse over towels.

← *March 28*

It occurs to me that I've never seen the movie *Titanic*. I don't know why, I just missed it. It was on cable the other night when I was flipping channels and I watched about five minutes before I got fed up with all the water and tilting and being handcuffed to pipes and such. I wonder how it ended, if they found a way to patch up the ship or something. Wouldn't that be an awesome alternate ending? Like maybe the crew passed out emergency bubble gum and everybody chewed a whole bunch and they used it to patch up the iceberg hole and all were saved and class differences erased and everyone lived happily ever after? No one ever said historical movies had to be historically accurate.

← *April 4*

This will be a short one, as I'm off to Iowa. The state that has a 3:1 vowel-consonant ratio. Either Iowa is an incredibly wealthy state (because, as we all know from watching

Wheel of Fortune, you have to buy the vowels), or they traded all of their entertainment options in exchange for all those vowels. I bet they are sorry now. (Speaking of geographic inequities, why does Africa have all the good animals? I know that Africa has plenty of other problems, and I am not trying to make light of those here, but damn. You got your lions, your elephants, your giraffes . . . all your major first-class grade-A star-quality zoo animals all on one continent. You go, Africa!)

The simplest explanation for why I am going to Iowa is that I have been invited to attend an ex-boyfriend's wedding, although the word "boyfriend" puts too light a spin on it. What actually transpired between us was quite a bit darker and more dysfunctional than that. However, he is still someone I enjoy and admire, so when his somewhat half-assed (late, hastily Xeroxed) wedding invitation arrived, I considered going, and LT, who apparently is just jonesing for a summertime adventure, seconded the motion. Iowa is an awkward distance from Chicago. It's strangely expensive to fly, since no one wants to go to Iowa, and all the flights are on creepy little deathtrap John Denver/JFK Jr. planes. But driving means five hours or so in the car, and the burden will be solely on LT. (I don't drive. If you ever rode with me back in the days when I did drive, you will recall exactly why I no longer drive. You will recall it with white-knuckled, eye-rolling, pants-wetting terror. I apologize if this diary entry has been a triggering mechanism for you.)

So stock up on the granola bars and bottled water, LT and Mimi are road-tripping to Iowa. Our car only has a cassette player, and I stopped buying tapes back around 1992, so the sounds of our trip will be distinctly old-skool. Which only seems appropriate for Iowa.

<del>——</del> *April 7*

Back from the Iowa trip. There sure was a lot of corn. The United States is just too huge. It's unmanageably huge. It's a huge, sparsely populated (for its size) place. The corn-sky-grass-highway, corn-sky-grass-highway montage was a bit bizarre and agoraphobic for me, to tell the truth.

However, the drive went a lot quicker than I thought it would and we were ahead of schedule for the wedding. Which was very good, since the alternator on the car blew up just as we were about twenty minutes from our hotel. (Don't ask me what an alternator is, but LT said it was an important bit of the car.) We made it to the hotel (these small towns have their advantages—we stayed in their "Executive Suite" at the ridiculously low price of seventy-nine dollars) and had our car fixed at the service station around the corner. For being an important bit of the car, an alternator is really not all that expensive. So if someone ever tells you that you need a new alternator, stay calm.

I ate two meals at a Perkins, because the food options in Coralville, Iowa, were somewhat limited, and now I never want to see another fried egg as long as I live. I enjoy a diner breakfast as well as the next girl, but two of those in two days was Grease Overkill. The wedding was nice—outdoors, mercifully short (I tend not to do well in direct sunlight), and no awkward scenes. The reception was a no-frills fried-chicken affair at an American Legion hall, which was interesting in its own way. I reunited with one of my favorite people, another former girlfriend of the groom, and we gabbed all night and were fabulous together and now I finally have a way to contact her that doesn't involve going through him. We arrived home on Sunday afternoon to a very cranky cat.

Also, since we had a lot of time in the car to talk, LT and I made some Important Life Decisions this weekend. We're going to chuck our jobs, sell our house, and hit the road as the world's first husband-and-wife Hall and Oates tribute band. However, we keep arguing about who gets to be Oates. I say I would look better in the mustache.

April 10

This morning I woke up to skunk smell, which seems to be a standard spring/summer thing in my neighborhood. I have to confess I sort of like skunk smell. Not that I want it splashed on my pulse points, made into a bath oil, or permeating my whole house, but the faint skunky aroma in the mornings is sort of neat. It is like: See! Who Needs Camping! We Have Plenty of Nature, Right Here in Filthy Chicago! My cat does not have similar warm and fuzzy feelings about the skunk smell. She stared at me all during breakfast and her expression clearly commanded me to *fix it*, and I said, "Sorry, no can do, but doesn't the skunk smell remind you of all the other nifty creatures on this planet? I kind of like it," and she just looked back and sent me the telepathic message, *You useless human.*

— *April 11*

HOW TO COME TO A PARTY AT MY HOUSE

1. Wear whatever you like. Hats, tuxedos, and false beards are all encouraged, separately or together.

2. You really don't have to bring anything. I know it is polite to ask, and I appreciate that politeness, but when I throw a party I am kind of a crazy control freak with the planning so I probably have it all covered. If your mother raised you in such a way that you absolutely cannot arrive empty-handed, wine (hint: I like pinot noir), tulips (hint: I like purple ones), or huge baggies of drugs are always welcome.

3. Say something nice about the food, because I am not always very confident of my domestic abilities.

4. Drink. Mingle. Don't wait to be introduced. Be funny. Here is a list of conversational topics to get you started: your favorite cheeses, scary things (nuns, clowns, midgets), stuff that sucks, weird sexual things you've done, drug stories (bonus points if they end up with you pantsless in a police station), caber tossing, your favorite popes in history (I've always enjoyed Pope Clement VI), famous people who you wouldn't mind having as your own personal fuckpuppet (again, Pope Clement VI for me), dinosaurs RRRAAARRR!, whether you believe that the declension in the Western post-Romantic mind from modernism to postmodernism can be understood as a shift from epistemological skepticism to ontological skepticism, the fact that a pig has a spiral penis, and the Incredible Hulk's bad haircut (seriously, did his mom cut his hair with a bowl?).

5. Conversational topics to avoid: work (funny stories are fine, but no one wants to hear the details of your spreadsheet wizardry), your gym routine, abortion/gun control/the death penalty/terrorism, what you did or didn't eat today, how everyone lusts after you, the amount of fabulously expensive electronic equipment you own, and platform snobbery (if I overhear even a tiny fragment of the Windows vs. Mac vs. Linux debate I'll slip a roofie in your drink, I swear). Also, anecdotes about how cute your pets or children are should be limited to five minutes or less.

6. Never, ever, insist that everyone stop drinking, talking, and generally having a good time in order to "play a game." Playing games is fine, if it is that sort of party. Or there can be a subgroup of game players within a larger party. But you are not the Camp Counselor of the party, to be demanding that the partygoers do this or that.

7. Be a good drinker: no vomiting, no wanton destruction, no unwanted groping of fellow guests. Dirty jokes, comic antics, flirtation, and slightly slurred stream-of-consciousness blather are encouraged, however. If things do get out of hand, you are welcome to spend the night. I have plenty of couch space.

8. Remember, your hostess sets the tone. So, if I am wobbling about like Dorothy Parker on a bad night, consuming superhuman quantities of gin, kissing just about everyone on the mouth, coming dangerously close to setting you on fire with my freely-gestured-with cigarette, and cracking wise about all and sundry, that gives you free license to completely let your hair down. And if at any point I drop into a kung fu stance, that is a clear signal that all bets are off. (For some reason I tend to make with the martial arts poses when I get very drunk.)

⟵ *April 14*

On the train this guy was staring at me, almost in a "do I know you" kind of way. I ignored it for a while and kept reading, but every time I glanced up he was still looking at me, and by now it had gone past "do I know you" and was just uncomfortable and weird. I was in the mood for sociological interpersonal experiments, so the next time I looked up and saw that he was still at it I stared back, expressionlessly and kind of aggressively, and we made eye contact for a few long seconds, and then still completely expressionless I slowly stuck one finger in my nose, staring at him the whole time. It worked like a charm, he immediately looked away and resolutely read his paper all the way downtown.

⟵ *April 16*

Hypothetically, if you were asked to go to a hypothetical meeting smack in the middle of a very busy day, and the person in charge of the meeting had recently been to a management seminar that had obviously damaged his or her brain, and instead of discussing any actual business or resolving any actual issues that person had asked you to prepare a list of your "triumphs" of the past year and the "areas of refocus" for the year ahead for discussion, would you want to scream? Would you want to go Bruce Lee on all of upper management's sorry asses? Would you at least want to put your diminutive combat boot through a wall? I think you might. Hypothetically. Let's see: Triumphs of the Past Year: I managed not to stab anyone. Areas of Refocus: Sharpen the stabbing knife.

April 17

I'm on the elliptical trainer thing at the gym (I know it's hard to picture me exercising, but shut up. Don't you want my sweet, supple ass to stay sweet and supple? Well alrighty then), sweating and puffing as I make my elliptical way toward my fitness goal (which is very modest: my goal is to be Not Quite So Flabby. Basically I have a potato-shaped torso—well, okay, maybe more of an elongated yam—and feeble, sticklike arms and legs. Do you remember that science project where you prop a sweet potato up on toothpicks so its lower half is in a jar of water? That's me. I am the sweet potato with toothpicks on the sides. In case you are slow, I will spell it out: the sweet potato is my torso and the toothpicks are my limbs. By the way, what was that science project supposed to teach you?)

One more clarification and then I swear we'll get started. I used the present tense up there in a pretentious, writerly way. I am not this minute sweating and puffing on the elliptical trainer.

Tray tables up? Carry-on items stowed in the overhead bins or under the seat in front of you? Good.

The elliptical trainer has merit. It's kind of fun, and I like the fact that it is a very strange movement pattern that you could never do on the ground. Unless you were in zero gravity or something. (While we're speaking of space, did you know that Uranus is the only planet that spins on its side? All other planets spin clockwise or counterclockwise. Heh. Uranus.)

Could somebody FedEx me some Ritalin? I don't seem to be able to stay on topic today.

The gym has a whole lot of televisions. With the closed captioning, or apparently you can wear a Walkman and tune it to a certain frequency to hear the television. That seems like a lot of effort for crappy daytime TV, plus I enjoy talk shows with closed captioning, because there's nothing like trying to follow the poorly typed threads of really stupid people's conversations. It is like being in an Internet chat room, only on TV! Recently I have witnessed the following amazing topics on TV talk shows, while at the gym. I believe these are all from *Jenny Jones*, which is usually on when I go to the gym, which is odd because I go at all different times. Maybe the gym is an alternate universe where *Jenny Jones* is always on television. Mommy, I'm scared.

An episode wherein the audience and a panel of "judges" tried to guess whether the giant freak boobs of the guests were real or fake. Sigh.

An episode where skanks accused their skank friends of being too skanky. I think it was even titled "Girl, You're Too Skanky!" or something like that. For instance, one exotic dancer slagged off her friend, who was also an exotic dancer, for "going too far," or, I guess one could say, dancing too exotically. In essence, she claimed that her nude dancing around a pole was tasteful and artistic, but her friend's nude dancing around a pole was slutty. The friend hotly denied this.

An episode titled "Player or Chickenhead?" where the audience judged, and held up signs indicating their judgment, whether someone was a player or a chickenhead. I think I have a handle on the definition of "player," but chickenhead? What the hell? And of course it was impossible to deduce from context, between the garbled closed captioning and the sweat dripping in my eyes. I wish someone would clue me in to the meaning of "chickenhead." Apparently it is not a chicken's head.

And finally, the loveliest little moment of all my at-the-gym talk show moments: when they (they, you know, they) introduce someone in a talk show, his or her name usually appears on screen, with a little summary underneath, such as "Ginger: Thinks She's All That" or "D'W'ay'ne: Pimping His Baby's Momma," and so forth. I glance up at the screen this particular day and see the words "Greg: Has No Clue." I couldn't have put it better myself.

◂— *April 20*

Dear Alley Assholes,

Thank you for staying true to your beliefs that the alley is a sort of expressway and that it is totally appropriate to roar up and down it in the early morning hours. I especially appreciate your thoughtfulness in the way that you do not stop or slow down or even look both ways at alley junctures, but instead continue at your same rate of speed while sounding the horn. That way, when me or some other unsuspecting pedestrian is dragged under your giant SUV tires, we will be able to hear the melodious tones of your car horn as we expire, which will undoubtedly be a great comfort to us.

Dear Man Who Shadowed Me All the Way Down the Aforementioned Alley Last Night,

Although I am a fearless urban warrior girl, and a master of the don't-fuck-with-me walk, and am very rarely worried about anyone in my neighborhood, I have to offer my sincere thanks, sir, for walking exactly behind me and in my blind spot for the entire length of the alley. Most men are aware of the somewhat-undeserved reputation their gender has for menace, and, when walking in a darkish alley behind a waifly chick in a beret and mary janes, will either speed up and overtake her or drop way back so she doesn't have a chance to feel threatened. When I glanced back and realized that, as an Orthodox Jew, you are statistically and demographically rather unlikely to mug or assault me, I felt a little better, but still, please, show some common sense.

Dear Chicago Dental Works,

Thank you for your animatronic LED readout sign, which I saw from the bus, that says GET A HEALTHY AND HAPPY SMILE FOR 2003 and featured the cutest, most adorable, handsomest, happy tooth I have ever seen in my life. If an electronic rendering of a smiling tooth can be "dashing," he was that too—he just was all jaunty and smiling in a Cary Grant/William Powell sort of way, and I think I am in love.

Dear Woman Who Every Single Day on My Bus Takes Seven Blocks to Fumble in Her Purse and Eventually Find Her Transit Card,

There are these things called pockets. They are very useful.

Dear Undergarments,

What went wrong? I thought we were getting along great. But today I get to work, seriously needing to be in the bathroom after drinking eight cups of tea, and discover that you, Tights, have developed a hole, somewhere near the crotch area. It is not a huge hole, but your spandexy nature means that the hole could easily enlarge, and I would rather not be wearing crotchless tights at work (where it is highly inappropriate) or on the street (where it is currently unseasonably cold). I suppose I will be buying tights at lunchtime.

And Brassiere! What did I do to piss you off? Because I am sitting here typing along and feeling a minor discomfort in the boob area, but thinking not much of it, and then I happen to lean way down to plug in the teapot and end up looking down my own shirt (hubba hubba) and I notice the giant wire sticking up out of you. I had to wiggle out of you in my office with the door closed and stuff you in my bag, and now today is officially Unfettered Bosom Friday. Did you coordinate this with Tights? To have all my underwear fall apart at once? You guys are sneaky, I don't know if I can trust you anymore.

Dear Café Typhoon,

I bought one of your maki rolls for a late lunch, and are you hiring the handicapped to roll maki these days? Or are your chefs just depressed and alienated and don't see the point of their existence? Your maki is rolled so loosely and sloppily that even picking it up to dip into the soy sauce sent all the ingredients unspiraling into a vortex of disorder. I ordered os-hinko maki, not entropy maki.

Dear Brain Chemicals,

I would appreciate if whichever one of you is responsible for the inappropriate welling-up of tears would lay off a little. Here is a partial list of the things that have gotten me choked up this past week: seeing footage of a women's college basketball team celebrating, with big smiles and sisterly hugging and total jubilant positive energy everywhere; any television program or even news segment that includes a helper dog, like a bomb-sniffing dog or a rescue dog (there is something so stupidly touching about a dog that just wants to help you); seeing the words "I understand" in print, particularly in an e-mail or instant message from a friend; and little kids singing to themselves.

Dear Spinach, Feta, and Imported Black Olives,

Thank you for inspiring my husband to use you in a totally amazing pasta dish last night. Isn't it wrong of him to cook on his own birthday? I thought so. But you tasted so right.

⟵ *April 23*

THIS IS A PUBLIC SERVICE MESSAGE

Please don't fuck with people in the morning when they are majorly blood-sugar-crashing and need food. I get to work, work for a while, then realize I am starving to death, and start to heat up some water for instant oatmeal. Then I get an e-mail with the subject line: "Come to my office for birthday treats!" Hooray! I think. I am saved! Since I am seriously shaky and mumbly and light-headed, oatmeal would be the more stable and level-headed nutritional choice, but who can resist the spike in goofiness that would accompany eating a gooey brownie or icing-covered doughnut with a cup of tea? Certainly not me. So I open the e-mail to get the full story. It says, and I quote: "I brought treats for my birthday! Fruit leather and apple scones. Come on by!" Uh. Sure. Be right there. Not that I am totally anti-scone, but fruit leather seriously stretches the definition of "treat," and since I had irrationally gotten my blood-sugar hopes up I was crabby and wanted to reply *Bitch make with the chocolaty goodness before I bust a cap in your birthday-girl ass.* But I refrained.

⟵ *April 24*

My parents came recently to help us finish painting our bedroom. This was scheduled to take pretty much all day, so I e-mailed my mom and said, "Should I make us some lunch?" Now, something you should know is that my mom Does Everything Right. If she gives you a gift, it is not only perfectly wrapped but is probably also tied with raffia and has a cute homemade tag. If she makes you lunch, it has several delicious items and cloth napkins and a special dessert. She has always worked, and she is not some crazy uptight Martha Stewart person, but she sure does like to Do Everything Right and firmly believes in the philosophy of Making Things Nice. As you know, your correspondent Mimi Smartypants likes to Do Everything While Just a Little Tipsy and firmly believes in the philosophy of Good Enough. So on one level I was kind of hoping that my mom would write back and say, "Oh, don't worry about it, I'll bring lunch" or "Let's just order a pizza in between coats of paint." Instead she said, "Sounds good!"

I tried to think of things I could make that were nice enough to feed my mom but that also allowed for as little preparation as possible, and I ended up with a pasta salad and roasted vegetable sandwiches. I got the vegetables done early in the morning; mixed together some pesto, mayonnaise, and garlic; split open the hoagie rolls, and then started assembling sandwiches, with the thought that they could hang out in the refrigerator while we painted. Boy howdy! I thought. What an excellent little lunch-making girl I am!

By the time I had assembled sandwich #2, it was as if the serotonin plughole had been yanked out of my brain bathtub, and every happy moment I had ever experienced was spiraling away along with a bunch of soap scum and wet leg hair. *Making sandwiches is very depressing to me, for some reason.* I was thinking dark thoughts and nearly weeping onto the hoagie rolls. (Here is your sandwich, sir. I moistened it with my tears.) Now I know I should never have a large brood of children or work in a deli. Also, now I know why people who *do* work at delis look like that. I would not be surprised if Franz Kafka, Woody Allen, or Morrissey had worked at a deli. Hey, maybe they all worked together! At the same deli! Forget that Kafka died in 1924 and just go with me on this!

Morrissey: I have an appointment tomorrow to get my hair heightened. Can someone switch with me and work noon to six?

Woody Allen: Ah, oh, eeh, oh, um, this is pretty short notice, really . . .

Franz Kafka: Guys, I just saw a big cockroach in the storeroom. Really big.

Well, at least the bedroom is a now a lovely shade of pistachio green, and I managed not to stick my head in the oven.

← April 26

My only anecdote today is that someone needs to come be Encyclopedia Brown with me and solve the mystery of why my upstairs neighbor sings the national anthem (poorly) nearly every day, sometime between six and seven in the evening. Is she being whipped into a patriotic frenzy by war coverage on the national news? Is she practicing for baseball season? It is truly weird, and it tends to happen while LT and I are eating dinner. Now we are actually start-

ing to listen for it, and when it happens we have this routine where we salute our food.

◄ *April 29*

I went out to see this band last night, and observing the
local nightlife indie-rock dirty-hair scene led me to this
question re: "cool" . . . why is it that certain tall (invariably
tall) women can get away with wearing strange acetate
nightgown-type things with weird little sweaters and
bizarre grandma shoes and they look "cool"? Whereas I, in
the same clothing, would look like a mental patient?
Hmmm? Any thoughts on "cool"? Are you "cool"?

◄ *May 1*

My friend Sam and I were speculating recently on what the
Queen (of England) keeps in her purse. She's always carrying around this little pocketbook, but what could she
possibly require? I think it would be too freaky to use
money that had a picture of your own face on it. Maybe
breath mints. And a sewing kit.

The place where Sam and I were speculating was Bar
Louie. Normally I hate Bar Louie, because it is full to the
brim with khakis and cell phones and big-ass diamond en-
gagement rings and other accoutrements that belong to the
sort of folk who are Not My People. (I like to hang wit' my
peeps, you know what I'm sayin'?) That said, it is convenient to work, and it can be tolerable if you go very early

(drink early, drink often) and leave the minute it starts to get horrible. (It goes without saying that we are talking about the original Bar Louie here, the one on Chicago Avenue. Yes, it's a mini-chain. I told you it was dreadful.)

That was a very long preamble. Anyway, when in the course of human events it becomes necessary for a beer-drinking woman with a bladder the size of a thimble (and that would be me) to go to the bathroom in said Bar Louie, there is often a wait. Because it is the sort of bathroom that is for only one person. So I haul my ass off the bar stool to go to the john and indeed someone is using it and there's a chick ahead of me. And she's making all those little need-to-pee movements, and we notice that there's no one in the men's, and she goes, "Will you hold the door for me?" Of course I will. Sisterhood is powerful and all that.

She finishes, comes out, (remember that there is STILL a wait for the women's john) and goes, "Thanks, bye!" leaving me standing there.

Did I miss something? Is it not understood that you hold the door for her, then she holds the door for you? Was that not just rude?

I've ranted this story since to many people, and only my female friends get as pissed off as I was. I mean, my male friends agree that it sucked, but it doesn't seem to offend them on a personal level.

— *May 3*

I recently canceled my gym membership, because I realized I hated it. I hated every damn minute of every infrequent gym visit, and eventually my visits became so infrequent that I just stopped kidding myself and never went back. If my body requires more exercise than yoga and walking around the city and dancing all alone in the house like a dork, then my body and I are just going to have to have a little chat, because that is not going to happen. Do you hear me, body? I am not kidding around. Anyway, the gym of course sent me tons of mail with offers to renew the membership, all of which I ignored, and then yesterday I received a call at work. This uptalking, unbearably perky woman, whose ponytail and sports bra were somehow conveyed by her very voice, says "Hi? I am calling from Gorilla Sports?"

I don't say anything. What is there to say? Was that supposed to be a question? I don't know, *are* you calling from Gorilla Sports? Why don't you walk outside and look at the sign?

All those step-aerobics classes have taught Ponytail Voice one thing though: *Never quit.* So she bravely presses on: "We noticed that you didn't renew your membership?"

"Yup, that's right!" I say, and because I am in a weird mood I affect a sort of down-home aw-shucks cornpone accent. "I sure didn't! Renew my membership, that is! That is one thing I sho-nuff did not do!"

This makes her a little more subdued, and possibly frightened. In a smaller voice she asks, "Can I ask why? Don't you like us anymore?"

"Aw sugar, it ain't that," I said. "I just have a few complaints about the gym, that's all!"

Now this she can handle. Miss Buns of Steel has been through some customer-service training seminars in her time, that is for damn sure. She wants to know what my complaints are, and she will totally for real pass them on to upper management. Isn't that, like, totally tubular?

Me again: "For one thing, you people call yourselves Gorilla Sports but I ain't never seen not one gorilla in there! No gorillas on the treadmill, no gorillas in the kickboxing class, and not a single gorilla over on the free weights, and honey, if there is one thing a gorilla loves it is heaving those free weights around. Why, I ain't never seen nothing but human primates in your whole gosh-darned facility, excuse my language! No spider monkeys in the locker room, even! You should totally employ spider monkeys to bring towels to people, that would rule." (By this point I had kind of forgotten to keep using my Southern accent, but oh well.)

Quadriceps Queen said, "Okay . . . I will pass that on . . ." in practically a whisper. I thanked her. End of Act I. Now I have to find some spies who belong to that gym, and find out how they like the towel-bringing spider monkeys.

 *May 4*

THE THREE AND ONLY THREE INSTANCES
IN WHICH I WISH I WERE A MAN

1. Gas station bathrooms.

2. When I want to have a drink by myself in a bar, because there's something nice about decompressing with a beer and a good book in a quiet neighborhood bar, and I think there must be something about being female and alone in a bar that makes everyone assume that you must be desperate to make conversation, so people like to interrupt you ("Hey, whatcha reading?") and if you don't smile pretty and answer politely they think to themselves "What a bitch," but if you do you're trapped talking to Joe Six-Pack who now thinks you are either (a) his buddy or (b) available. If a man walked into a bar (hey, sounds like a joke!), ordered a beer, and started reading, people would find him either dashing and intellectual and mysterious or eggheady and weird, depending on the bar, but I guarantee no one would repeatedly bother him.

3. At formal events, because it would be so much easier just to throw on a suit or a tuxedo than to try and decipher the invitation like some kind of Rosetta stone: "Okay, formal. But how formal? Floor-length formal? Gloves formal? Dinner and dancing formal? And what sort of shoes? Fuck, I need to go shopping."

← *May 7*

I go to Subway occasionally for lunch, and purchase what LT calls a "condiment sandwich"— cheese and vegetables only. One of the sandwich makers is a strange and jovial guy. I'm not sure if he gives everyone shit or just me, but he's always fooling around, and so when I go to give my spiel (no mayonnaise, no tomatoes, no hot peppers, but everything else) he's teasing me like a big brother, "Okay, no mustard, right? Extra tomatoes, right?" I'm usually good-humored about it but after the third or fourth comment of this nature I said,

"Look, why are you busting my balls?" and found that it's just about possible to induce a seizure in a Subway employee by making him laugh so hard that he staggers backward from the sandwich counter with iceberg lettuce dripping from his plastic-glove hands. I swear to god, it just slipped out. Too much *Sopranos*, probably.

May 10

FOUR THINGS I CAN SEE OUT MY OFFICE WINDOW RIGHT NOW

1. The Hancock Building, and a bunch of other buildings that don't have names
2. Three construction cranes
3. A big gray SUV exiting a parking garage
4. A white plastic bag caught in an updraft, sailing around in circles

FOUR OF THE MANY CLASSES OFFERED AT THE UNIVERSITY OF ME

1. Advanced Topics in Overthinking and Obsession
2. Hair-Twirling and Cuticle-Chewing Seminar
3. The Art of the Nap
4. You Must Read Everything: Independent Study with Gargantuan Reading List

FOUR THINGS I INVOLUNTARILY LEARNED FROM THE YUPPIE BUSINESSMAN ON THE TRAIN WITH THE BOOMING, RESONANT VOICE, BECAUSE OF COURSE IT IS VITALLY IMPORTANT THAT WE ALL HEAR HIS CELL PHONE CONVERSATIONS

1. He used to think that society was a sort of meritocracy, and that how smart and creative you were and how hard you worked mattered, but now he realizes that "it's who you know." (Note: this realization didn't seem to bother him in the least.)

2. Pete is an idiot. Pete didn't copy John on that report. You can't trust Pete. Pete is going to get a new asshole ripped when he gets to work.

3. Hurry up, because his phone is almost out of battery power. He should be there in about fifteen minutes.

4. He can't have lunch on Monday because he's flying to Denver to meet with those assholes at the branch office. But he and you should get together the week after that, for a drink or something.

FOUR BEVERAGES I HAVE ALREADY CONSUMED TODAY, BECAUSE VARIETY IS THE FREAKING SPICE OF LIFE

1. Earl Grey tea
2. Water
3. Diet Pepsi
4. Cranberry-grape 100% juice

— *May 12*

There is a restaurant near the office that has a dish I like. It is udon noodles with lots of bok choy and mushrooms and other green leafy things. It is vegetarian and it is nice. On the menu it is called "Shanghai Noodle."

One fine day I place a phone call to this restaurant, for takeout. I order Shanghai Noodle. When I go to pick it up, the guy at the counter says, "We don't have Shanghai Noodle anymore. When you want to order Shanghai Noodle, order Crispy Sesame Chicken without the chicken. It's the same thing."

If it's the same thing, would it have killed them to keep that one extra line of type on the menu advertising Shanghai Noodle? It's not like they got rid of Shanghai Noodle entirely, they just added some chicken. Or, alternately, they could add an even tinier line of type to the menu under "Crispy Sesame Chicken" that says "without chicken" and the different price.

Okay. Fine. It seems kind of twisted to me, but *I will play your silly game.* So a few months later I call up and order Crispy Sesame Chicken Without the Chicken. When I go to pick it up, the counter guy teases me, "What's the matter? Don't like chicken?" That made me angry. "Look," I said. "I am just trying to use *your* stupid terminology. In an effort to *communicate.* It is not my fault that your menu signs and signifiers are all *obfuscated* and *hopeless.* You people make me talk in your strange special code just to get some damn lunch."

Maybe it's political. Maybe they had just fired a guy from

Shanghai and they wanted no reminders of him on the menu. Who knows. But I resent it, yes I do.

⟵ *May 18*

The weather here is sliding into that danger zone where I start to panic, because soon it will be too warm for black tights and turtleneck sweaters and other aspects of my urban hijab, and I know I bitch about this every time the mercury rises but I seriously have no warm-weather clothes, and whenever I attempt to buy some I end up fleeing the retail environment in horror at the boob slings and handkerchiefs and foot-exposing sandals that the fashion world seems to expect me to wear. My booty may be fine, my booty may be all that and a family-sized bag of chips, my booty may bring certain carefully selected grown men to their knees, begging me please, but the entire world does not need to see my booty, no matter how warm the weather, thank you very much the end.

⟵ *May 19*

Do you have someone in your family who is a nut for taking photographs? Do you sometimes wonder if you remember actual events in your childhood or if you actually just remember the photograph? I know I have the snapshot memories, but I do have ones that don't have anything to do with photographs, like the time I remember realizing that I was a distinct entity who by necessity apprehended the world through my own limited sensory organs. This was at around five years old, going for a walk on the golf course behind my grandparents' house, which is interesting because I ended up having a mild acid flashback on that very same golf course many years later (golf course as quicksand, me sinking, slogging through fairway up to my waist, and everything with a gorgeous watery violent tinge to it). I guess that particular golf course was some sort of brain-energy nexus for me.

Anyway, this was supposed to be about memory and photographs. Kat and I had a conversation recently about school photographs and how they are often relied on, by lazy or unsentimental families, as a shorthand record of the changes in a kid. Also about how everyone has one particular school photograph that they can identify as the definitive visual evidence of their Severely Ugly Awkward Stage. Mine came in third grade. I am missing teeth (and not the cute ones), I have big black plastic Buddy Holly glasses frames (what kind of ghetto optician thought that would work on a seven-year-old girl?), and I have long dark Wednesday Addams braids with that dorky thick red yarn on the ends. And some kind of grayish-brown polyester dress with a Peter Pan collar, like a leftover orphan from a low-budget production of *Annie*. It was a hard-knock life, indeed.

Photographs don't work as memories but memories don't work as memories either. The minute you say "I am going to remember this in precisely this way" you are doomed; your mind (or my mind, anyway) begins the process of smoothing the edges, rearranging the scene, blurring the all-important sensory impressions, until you can perfectly recreate the *idea* of the memory of the event (the kiss, the desert at night, the car crash) but you have nothing approximating a perfect copy of the event. Maybe memory is not meant to be a perfect copy anyway, but something entirely else (which is probably part of the reason people take photographs in the first place). However, I sometimes find it frustrating that the Internal Film Production Editor of my brain insists on narrating, cutting, and splicing, even if ever so slightly.

◂— *May 22*

Why did some Martin Luther of Garbage nail a moldy piece of pizza, encased in a plastic bag, to a garage door a few buildings down from mine? I see this in the alley every morning, and I note the progress of the pizza's decay, and I wonder. Science project? Voodoo fetish? A warning from the Sicilian mafia? Good-luck talisman? Will someone come pick it up at some point? ("Listen, I have to go out for a while, but I'll nail your moldy pizza to the door. Just come by and get it whenever.")

◂— *May 23*

Today marks the fourth day in a row I have forgotten to pick up my dry cleaning. This despite the fact that yesterday I used as a bookmark a large piece of paper that said, *Pick up the dry cleaning you dumbshit dumb-ass loser*. And yet I walked right past the dry cleaners and didn't think of it again until midnight. Maybe my subconscious doesn't respond well to name calling. Today I will try a note that says, *You are such a good person that you will no doubt remember to get the dry cleaning without fail.* I hope that works, because my supply of even vaguely professional-looking work clothes is dwindling fast. I may have to go to work tomorrow in a leftover Wonder Woman costume, wearing my bedsheets like a cape.

 *May 26*

AN INTERVIEW WITH THE CRAZY GUY
WHO RIDES MY BUS*

mimismartypants: Hi there!

CGWRMB: Motherfuck! (pounds on window)

MS: You know, I see you every day and you are perpetually muttering and angry about something. What gives? It's a beautiful day.

CGWRMB: Don't hit your sister! Don't hit your sister! Don't hit your sister! Don't hit your sister!

MS: You are absolutely right. Friends come and go, but sisters are forever. Physical abuse certainly could ruin that relationship.

CGWRMB: Everybody off the bus!

MS: No.

---

*Imagined, because I'm kind of chickenshit when it comes to the violently insane

CGWRMB: Everybody off the bus!

MS: No. It's not my stop yet. I've had a long day, I'm not walking twelve extra blocks home.

CGWRMB: Ahhhhhhh! Blarrrggggg! Fwwwoooomahhh! (makes exploding noises with mouth)

MS: Thank you for taking the time to speak with us today.

Although I do prefer to sit where I can keep an eye on CGWRMB, I think he's pretty harmless. He is kind of an interesting character, actually, since he is very clean and well-dressed and is obviously coming from somewhere at the same time every day, and his outbursts are not classically Tourettic but rather seem to stem from some sort of private dialogue.

◢ May 27

MY ONLY SNAPPY COMEBACK OF THE DAY

Scene: I am at the fancy sandwich place. The fancy sandwich place has many combination sandwiches, and you order by fancy sandwich number (for instance, the roasted vegetable one that I like is the #62, which is kind of mysterious as there do not seem to be anywhere near sixty-two combinations). The fancy sandwich counter is open to customer visibility, so I am watching the sandwich girl load up the roasted vegetables and she starts to put the fresh tomatoes on there too, and don't ask me why *fresh* tomatoes are even included in a *roasted* vegetable sandwich, but I would rather not have them included because I have Tomato Issues. It's a texture thing. "Can you leave off the tomatoes?" I asked politely. Her plastic-glove hand hovered over the tomato container and she said, "Uh, we don't allow substitutions."

"No, of course not, that would be anarchy," I replied. "Carry on."

← May 30

We did not have a dishwasher growing up, and I think I'm getting the hang of it now, which is good since my one and only previous experience with using a dishwasher was a disaster. Back in college, when LT and I were dating, his dad went out of town for a weekend and we took the opportunity to spend it at his place, sort of playing house and getting away from campus for a while. On Saturday LT went to run an errand, and I'm all "la la la," being the happy homemaker and shit, and decided to be helpful and run the dishwasher. Which I did not know how to use. I grabbed the liquid soap off of the sink and *filled* up that little dispenser, shut the door, pushed some buttons, and went to another part of the house to read, feeling very pleased with myself.

Needless to say, when I came back into the kitchen, it was like being at some poorly designed rave. The suds were up to my waist, and the machine was still churning. I started flailing around with towels and mops, which were woefully unequipped for a task of that magnitude, and cursing at the top of my lungs as I tried to wade through the wall of suds to get to the dishwasher to turn it off.

In the middle of all this LT came home and stood there in the doorway looking at my wet, sudsy, crazy situation. I was speechless myself, since, hello, I came for the weekend and then I basically ruined your ancestral home. Then LT turned to me and said the only thing one could say at that point:

"Okay, Lucy. 'Splain."

I love that man.

◄ *June 9*

You know these little capsules that you put in warm water and a foam animal emerges? Do you? Well, get some. And do them inside your mouth, with beer. This was great fun recently, at a bar with Kat I had one in my mouth, almost finished exploding, when a guy sat down near us and said, "Hi" in that I'm-going-to-chat-you-up way. I held up a finger to say, "Wait a minute," leaned over, and spat a foam brontosaurus onto the bar top. He didn't stay long. It was beautiful.

◄ *June 10*

HOW TO EAT M&M'S LIKE MIMI SMARTYPANTS

Get the small bag. Anything larger than the standard vending-machine size is too overwhelming. It goes without saying (but apparently it doesn't) that you can't eat M&M's on the run. Sit down somewhere. Why are you in such a hurry anyway? Sit or stand in front of a hard flat horizontal surface (kitchen table, desk, bar). Now tear open the bag and pour the M&M's out onto that surface. (If your surface looks none too clean, you can always lay down a napkin or paper towel first; however, if it seems "clean enough," I recommend you take your chances with the germs because the skittery sliding sound and feel of M&M's on a hard flat horizontal surface is part of the overall experience.) Now separate the M&M's by color. Each color in its own little fiefdom. Before you protest, listen well: now is not the time for your convoluted metaphors about world harmony and integration. This is merely candy we have in front of us, not a multiethnic neighborhood, and a simple color-sorting algorithm is what we are after. Here is the fun part. The fun part is coming now.

THE FUN PART

You need to decide on a system. In what order will you consume each colored pile? There are many options here: Roy G. Biv, Least-Pleasing Color to Most-Pleasing Color (this one is unscientific and thus not as desirable), Backward Alphabetical by Color Name,* or my favorite, Statistical Significance. That is, eat the color pile with the fewest M&M's, and then eat the one with the next fewest M&M's, and so on until you reach the pile with the most M&M's, which is always the dark brown pile: *Yeah! Go dark brown! Dark brown wins by virtue of its supersaturation of the M&M universe!* If two piles have the same number of M&M's you can use alphabetical as the tie-breaker: green before orange, for example.

---

*This is a modification/workaround of Alphabetical by Color Name, because to do it forward would mean that yellow would be last, and that cannot happen because yellow is bad.

Some people contend that you can just eat M&M's by the handful with no system and with no regard to color. I find these people alarming.

◄── *June 18*

Chicago is under water. It rained hard and complicatedly all night long, complete with some of the loudest thunder you ever heard in your life, and brief power outages that screwed up every clock in my house, and currently the sky's mouth is still set in a thin hard line and the sky looks like it is getting good and ready to throw another tantrum and rain for another six hours. Apparently the subway tunnels have flooded and all the morning trains had to be rerouted over the elevated bit, and all the extra train traffic meant that we literally inched around the Loop. Which wouldn't have been so bad, since I had stuff to read: the latest *New Yorker* and the last hundred pages or so of my biography of Hart Crane (who is turning out to be rather an asshole, and I am not nearly as impressed with the poetry as when I was an impressionable high school Romantic, so while I am trying to finish this book I keep thinking, *God just hurry up and kill yourself already*). Well, the slow train wouldn't have been so bad except for the guy next to me being so very *weird* and *chatty*. He was one of those people who felt the need to remark on everything. "Boy, this is some rain," he said. "Do you like Starbucks?" he asked. "I should call the office," he mused. "I'm going to be pretty late." And, practically facedown in my lap as he craned to see out of the rain-streaked El window, "Wow, look how dark the sky is!" Here are some responses I seriously considered making:

1. What am I supposed to say to inane comments like those?

2. Where are you from? We do not speak to strangers here.

3. Can't you see I am reading?

At one point (whygodwhy) he even attempted to personalize his blather. "Name's Jim. What's yours?" Arrgggh. Je m'appelle "Bite Me."

←*June 20*

I had to go to the bank. To get a money order for a stupid government office. I *hate the bank*. For me, major stress headaches and the bank go together like Muppets and fisting.

It is a toss-up between which place I hate more, the bank or the post office. *Let us test this theory in an unscientific way. Yea verily.*

1. The post office has surly government employees who basically cannot be fired, and they know it. All the employees at my post office have permanent sneers and they are also not too bright (as evidenced by the post office employee who asked me, "Is that a new country?" when I was trying to mail something to Yemen). Thus, the bank might have a bit of an edge when it comes to customer service. However, since the big banks are eating all of the smaller banks these days, eventually we will have one giant monopoly bank and the notion of customer service will go right out the window. Advantage: *bank* (for the time being).

2. You might be lucky enough to be in the bank during a holdup, which would at least relieve the tedium of standing in line as you lie down on the floor with your hands in plain sight, not moving if you know what's good for you. But there's always the chance that one of the postal employees will, well, "go postal," and he/she might yell entertaining anti-governmental slogans while shooting up the place and might even take some hostages. In contrast, bank robbers simply want cash. Advantage: *post office*.

3. At the post office you usually leave empty-handed, except for maybe some stamps. At the bank you sometimes leave with money. It is usually your own money, unless you are one of the aforementioned bank robbers. Advantage: *bank*.

Long story tedious and mundane, I walk into the Bank One at Ohio and Michigan, thinking I am being very clever for going at a non-lunchy time, and I go upstairs to where the tellers are, and the line is about a mile long. The line is so long, and the people in line are so disgruntled, that a perky blond bank employee in a short skirt is dispatched to walk up and down the line and offer us cookies. (Note: they are crap cookies. They are the kind of cookies that are in the funeral home's Family Freak-Out and Illicit Smoking Area at wakes. All crumbly and gross with lurid pink powdered sugar on top.) Cookies don't help. More tellers working might help, and fewer people in line might help. The line also moves very slowly, and everyone in front of me seems to require something difficult, like maybe they are trying to withdraw money from a savings account belonging to their dead grandmother in Cuba. Or they are trying to exchange Confederate money for Estonian crowns. I had a simple (if irritating) money order thing. Yeah. I waited basically forever. I'm still there, in line at the bank, in a manner of speaking. Deep inside my soul, I am still in line at the bank.

← *June 23*

Violin? Oh that old piece of wood? I don't think I want to go back to my lessons for a while. Here are the reasons, with rebuttals in parentheses, because I can never ever stop second-guessing myself. If I stop second-guessing myself, I die! I am like a Shark of Doubt! Only instead of swimming forward, it's all about the self-doubt!

Reason #1: I am all busy. (Yeah. You are really busy. Two hours of couch or beer time could easily be converted into a violin lesson.)

Reason #2: I am kind of fed up with Paul's teaching methods, the way he is too quick to correct instead of letting me figure things out on my own, and the way he likes to play along with me during tricky passages, which does me no good at all since then I can't hear what I am doing. (You could let him know these things, since you are ostensibly a grown-up and are paying the guy, instead of just not calling him anymore.)

Reason #3: I have temporarily lost interest, to tell the truth. (The rebuttals to this are complicated . . . part of me is gleefully embracing the idea that I can simply *not do* what I don't want to do [a touch of Good Girl Syndrome? Who, me?], and part of me thinks that is not a good enough reason, and I should be forcing myself to continue my violin lessons, because I have been playing the violin off and on for twenty-five years now.)

Maybe I will quit the lessons temporarily, and continue to practice occasionally at home, when the mood strikes me, and of course continue to be a sassmouthy know-it-all when it comes to other people's violin playing. Like the elderly Asian man busking at Chicago and State, who flatly scrapes away on some Brahms thing and whoa he is bad. Whenever I wait for the subway there and he is doing his bit I almost want to say, "Excuse me, can you play your violin . . . better?"

◄—*June 24*

Last night I went to Delilah's with Kat, where we drank beer and made fun of people's bad tattoos. Quietly, behind their backs, in the most chickenshit way possible, of course. I was not looking to start fights with aging punk rockers. When I got home LT was busy prank calling the National Rifle Association. He had been watching TV and saw an 800 number on one of their infomercials. I gleefully joined in. When someone answered we would yell *"Soylent Green* is people!" or "Get your dirty hands off me, you goddamn dirty apes!" or other phrases relating to their spokesjerk, Charlton Heston. It was hysterical. Well, to us, anyway.

June 29

I've been away. And now I'm typing with only one hand. Yes, I done went and had the surgery for the bizarre wrist lump I have had for a year now, so I am no longer The Girl with the Ganglion Cyst. Thursday morning at early o'thirty I showed up at the outpatient surgery unit of Northwestern Hospital, and a few hours later the wrist lump was history.

A few highlights: Northwestern is a teaching hospital, so I had multiple residents asking me the same questions in the preoperative suite. They were all young guys, and I got sick of answering the question "What was the date of your last menstrual period?" with a staid "Um, it's going on now" (which it was), so to the last resident who asked I replied with a chirpy "Currently flowing, sir!" I think I scared him.

Finally some nurse anesthetist showed up to put some shots into my saline drip: alprazolam (generic name for Xanax: isn't the idea of a Xanax IV just wonderfully decadent? I could use one of those at work, sometimes) and fentanyl. LT got to stay with me until they took me away to the operating room, and after the shots went in the nurse person said, "Okay, do you feel sleepy yet?" and LT says I replied, "No, I feel fine" and then my eyes rolled back in my head like in cartoons and that was all she wrote. He was quite amused.

So now I have a messed-up hand. It's all swollen and yellow and ooogy, and I have a big stupid wrist brace on, which is supposed to keep me from flexing my wrist. My fingers and thumb are out, so I can sort of type and sort of print, and tie my shoes and all that, but I can't do anything that requires twisting. You would be amazed at how many activities of daily living require twisting. The biggies so far are those childproof caps on pill bottles and putting my hair in a ponytail. Very difficult.

Here's an observation that could only come from the swamp that is the brain of Mimi Smartypants: the incision is about three inches long, horizontally on the back of my wrist, and there's a black stitch that runs along its length, rather than back and forth. I think it looks like a coin slot in the back of my hand. If someone deposited a nickel in my hand I wonder what it could do.

⟵ *July 1*

There's a new, absolutely godawful subway musician at the Jackson Avenue Red Line stop: an older bearded guy with a boom box playing some boring R&B beat, and then he just moans, "*Jeeee-eeee-eeee-eeesus!*" over and over again with varying cadences and out-of-tune arpeggios. It sounds like someone is squeezing all the air out of him, and it is hellaciously loud, and it makes me want to drink paint thinner. Moaning Jesus Guy, please stop. Thanks.

THINGS I USED TO BELIEVE THAT TURNED OUT NOT TO BE TRUE

1. That sexual intercourse was always performed standing up.

2. That you should never peel the outer covering off a golf ball because inside is a poison gas that can seep out and kill your whole family.

3. That all humans were linked in a sort of meme pool/Jungian collective unconsciousness way and that there were no unbridgeable chasms between distinct phenomenological minds.

4. That wolverines roamed in every wooded area, hungry for little-kid flesh. And that wolverines can climb trees.

5. That it was incredibly expensive to have a key copied, and that it took days.

6. That the Other loves you for who you "really" are, not just for who you are in the context of your relationship with him or her. (Note: the loss of this belief did not produce as much despair as one might think: see 6a.)

6a. That the search for a core self, made up of unchanging and unshifting deeply true attributes, values, and beliefs, is a meaningful way to spend one's time.

7. That if I rode my tricycle fast enough, the wheels would leave the ground like airplane landing gear and I would take off into the sky.

8. That anyone of any importance would ever care what my standardized test scores were.

9. That I wouldn't be all that sad when my childhood dog died, since he was very old and I hadn't lived at home for years. (In reality I cried almost nonstop for two days.)

10. That, given a steady supply of beer and cigarettes, it is not really necessary to consume food.

← *July 5*

Like many of my fellow Americans, I spent part of Independence Day in the emergency room. Unlike many of them, however, my injuries were not caused by lighting fifty bottle rockets simultaneously or any other explosion-related stupidity. No, your friend Mimi, being the total spaz you know and love, managed to injure herself having a wholesome snack.

I love green apples (especially with that delicious caramel apple dip, conveniently sold in single-serving containers: whose brilliant idea was *that!* but I can't eat them out of hand, so I always use this apple sectioner device: basically a sort of two-handled bladed circle with spoked sections. You position it over the apple, press down *hard*, and the thing slices the whole apple into lovely little wedges.

The pressing down *hard* thing there is key. I am not sure precisely what happened, but somehow I managed to press the very sharp thing down *hard* into my thumb. Whump! Spurt, spray. Girlish shriek. (I'm still embarrassed about the girlish shriek part. Must learn to be more stoic in the face of blood.)

Speaking of blood. I later found out I had nicked an artery, which accounts for the sudden amazing gorefest. The kitchen looked like a crime scene. Blood on the cabinets, blood on the floor, blood on the counters, blood on the toaster. Several yards worth of bloody paper towels as I soaked through one layer after the other. You know how, when you cut yourself, it takes a minute for the blood to well up and spill out? Well, not so when you hit an artery. It jets out. Just in case you were wondering. (It's indicative of the way my mind works that, even in the middle of this trauma, I was noting this interesting phenomenon.)

Luckily LT was home, and boy howdy, what a guy. I think I should rent him out to people who think they are likely to have an emergency. He was very efficient in assessing the situation, was much more realistic than I about the need to go to the emergency room, and was very reassuring (kind of overly so, in fact: kept insisting I "sit down" and "keep calm" while he located shoes and car keys. I really was fine, if a bit grossed out by the whole affair).

So: six stitches. Six! In my tiny little thumb! Yes, it's the cursed left hand, the same one that suffered the wrist surgery. My hands are covered in scars, like a butcher's. And any plans I had to switch careers from editor to hand model are scuttled before they even got off the ground. Sigh.

Interesting side note: At the emergency room, I felt compelled to warn every nurse and doctor who peeled back my bloody bandages to get a look at the damage that the sight would be gross. As if they don't have plenty of experience with gross, way beyond my sliced-up thumb. Although it was gratifying to hear the doctor say, as he stitched, that the cut really was "quite deep"—everyone who's ever gone to the hospital with an injury has that weird self-conscious fear that their injury is not serious enough to warrant hospital attention. Mine was.

←—*July 10*

Last night I was out with Tom, and the bar was pretty crowded so he and I were slumped over in that weird, gray, strangely-low-to-the-ground couch by the pool table, and that couch always makes me nervous because no matter how crowded that bar gets it seems like *no one ever sits there* (except for us), which makes me wonder if every other patron knows something I don't. So we're sitting there, at eye level with people's knees, and there's this one girl wearing short pants and one of her legs is weird-looking. The skin was all shiny and smooth, and she was holding it in kind of a delicate fashion, strangely cocked behind her. I kept trying to see her other leg for comparison but it was too dark. Tom noticed it too, and whispered: "Does that girl have an artificial leg?"

"Maybe," I said. "I was noticing that too. She's standing funny and the ankle is vaguely plastic-like."

We tried to talk of other things but kept returning to the question of real leg vs. fake leg. "Crawl over there and poke it," he urged me.

"I am *not* going to get caught poking some stranger's leg. Besides, you couldn't crawl anywhere on this bar floor. You'd get mired in the La Brea tar pit of spilled beer and popcorn bits. Like a mastodon from the distant past."

I suggested going the brazen route of just asking her if

she had an artificial leg, but then we worried that if she did, she might think we were some kind of strange amputee fetishists, and if she didn't, she might think we were making fun of her in an obscure fashion. I'm still slightly obsessed with settling the question. Maybe a Missed Connection ad: Wednesday night, Goldstar, 10 P.M. You may have had an artificial leg. Call me.

⟵ July 13

Is language limiting or is it all we have? On really bad days I think about little kids learning to speak, learning to put labels on everything. At first, when you are small, things like the sky, light, and trees are so wide, so liquid, so limitless, so new to you, so directly experienced, and then you learn the words "sky" or "light" or "tree" and click, just like that, the liquid is curdled and the word is forever what you know and there's a brand-new box around what you see. And then the box gets filled up with associations, and the thing becomes the word the way the memory becomes the photograph. Of course there's no real alternative, and since I am a writer, a language freak, and a teeny bit Wittgensteinian I really don't mind so much, but remember, we are talking about how I feel on bad days. Sometimes words feel like a pocketful of rocks or crawl pointlessly across the page and I think: why do I even bother to try and talk to people? Why do I bother to communicate anything? Why can't we just be like animals and, I don't know, *pee* everywhere as a means of communication? Because this word thing is totally hopeless.

You know how sometimes you feel all beaten down by the city? Even if you have lived here practically your whole life, and you relish the crunching of crack vials under your feet and the rampant mayor-for-life political corruption and the shittiest sports teams who ever put on specialized sports equipment. Here's my theory: Chicago is like an emotionally abusive boyfriend, who will put you down in public and be mysteriously cold to you in private. Chicago will suddenly snap at you for nothing at all when you are finally in a good mood for once. And Chicago will put all kinds of obstacles in your path, and have godawful weather, and fix it so you can't go two lousy days without being treated to the sight of some hobo flamboyantly vomiting off an El platform. This will go on for weeks. And then, in classic emotionally abusive fashion, Chicago will conspire to treat you right. Chicago will do some small unexpected nice thing for you. You will be leaving work and there is the express bus right there! And it will be just about totally empty and you will get a seat on the lake side so you can watch the water as you zoom up Lake Shore Drive. Just as the bus pulls up to Loyola and you cross the street, your east-west connection arrives, and that's empty too, and you are making unbelievable time and the sunset makes even Devon Avenue, one of the most garbagey streets in the city, look nice.

God, I hate it when I get all second-person like that. It's so 1987.

So then I (me myself and I) am on the Devon bus and at one point I am the last person on the bus. A few stops before mine there is a red light and the bus driver is just sitting there, filling out paperwork, and we go through two traffic-light cycles without him moving. I don't know what the deal is, or why my Bartleby the Bus Driver suddenly prefers not to, but it is becoming annoying so I get up to leave, thinking I will just walk the rest of the way. When I stand he jerks upright, startled, and says, "Girl! You scared me! I didn't know anyone was still here! How long were you going to be quiet like that? You should have said something!" "I didn't want to be rude," I said. "I don't mind walking."

"No way, uh-uh," he replied. "You are on a *bus*. You are going to *ride*."

I liked that.

◂ *July 17*

This is my week to listen to semicrazy people talk out loud and then write down what they say. I am on the train and there is a disheveled man standing in the aisle and singing this song:

(incantatory blues style)

Lord, Lord, I am popcorn.
Lord, Lord, I am good to eat.
Lord, Lord, I am buttercrunchy.
Lord, Lord, a popcorn treat.

Who popped this popcorn?
Who popped this popcorn?
Who popped this popcorn?

(dramatic pause)

Jesus did!

I can't help it, I just start giggling helplessly. The seed/kernel/exploding-with-blessedness-and-becoming-a-delicious-salty-snack metaphor is just too much for me, and I like thinking about Jesus standing by the microwave watching the souls of all his little believers explode and watch out for that steam when you open the bag, Jesus! Also, I have always appreciated the little ditties of the subway crazies. Someone should come out with a CD: *Songs in the Key of Subway Crazy*. I would totally buy it. So I am laughing and the woman next to me glances over at me from her book like *I* am the big weirdo, and I say, "I'm sorry, that was really funny." She turns back to her book without even acknowledging me and I want to scream, *Did you not hear that guy's popcorn song? Because it ruled! And you just missed a beautiful moment of public transportation!*

← *July 18*

I have achieved a new level of hungoverness. Actually it's not that terrible, it just seems that way because I'm at work. Sucking down tea and chomping on a bagel in an effort to become this side of normal.

Calling in was not an option, because my drinking was done in a work setting, at a function for editorial last night, and to call in would mean that everyone would know why I was calling in. Which is not an option. Because I may not have glowing skin (but rather ashen and clammy), bright twinkling eyes (but rather purple-ringed and sunken), or a charming and friendly demeanor (but rather surly and snarling), but I do have my pride.

The weirdest feature of this particular hangover is a slight trend toward hysteria: I was on the phone with Sam and I started giggling pretty hard at something I said (because I am the funniest person I know) and couldn't exactly manage to stop. I feel like the top of my head could come off at any moment and I could collapse into random giggles, shouting, and hebephrenia, and they would have to take me away in a straitjacket and on a handtruck like Hannibal Lecter. And wouldn't that make a grand spectacle for my coworkers? Talk about not having pride.

Despite all this, it is a lovely day here in Chicago. If only I were alive to enjoy it.

I washed my hair this morning, not because I needed to, but because of the bar smell. Let's talk about hair for just a moment. Now that I have joined the ranks of the Long-Haired, it has come back to me (for I have not been long-haired before this since college) that you do not wash your hair every day when said hair is long. Now all you short-haired folks (and I was one of you for years, let's not forget) are going to be all like, "Ewww!" but hold on a second. Hair gets oily because of the scalp. When you have long hair, the majority of the hair is very far away from the scalp. Hence it is not dirty as often as short hair.

I vaguely remember this from the last time I had a bunch o' hair, but I had forgotten it until recently. I was washing my hair every day, and occasionally thinking, "Damn, why does my hair look like crap? Why are we so dry and frizzy and static-y all the time?" Then I remembered. So it is every other day for this girl from now on, for as long as the long hair lasts, unless of course there are gross bar smells to be gotten rid of.

And this revelation is revelatory only to me. Because, like I told you, I am hungover. And slightly hysterical. Very close to the edge now, people.

Don't cross me.

◄— *July 20*

A certain Crabby Person just called me up and left a long snarky message (thankfully I was away) about all the things that we here in publishing had done wrong and basically just implied how freaking stupid we were, when really it's a simple case of my not being able to read minds, and if you want something done on your manuscript you simply must e-mail, or fax, or telephone, or skywrite, or otherwise convey your concerns to me. Stupid jerk.

I tried a new brand of tea (Joy, from Tazo Teas) that was just not good, although the label said all the right things (a blend of black, green, and oolong teas). I think they got the blend wrong, because it was all funny (peculiar, not ha ha) and burnt-tasting. Regardless, I drank way too much of it and ate a bunch of chocolate as my midmorning snack, and I'm listening to the Pixies which always makes me slightly crazed (in a good way), and about a billion things have happened (up to and including the Crabby Person) since I arrived at work today. So I'm a little tense.

And manic. I think I can feel my ponytail twitching. In fact, I went upstairs to Kevin's office looking for a certain proof, and while he searched for it I just couldn't stand still any longer so I did a little hopping dance. I think I frightened him.

—July 23

Remember that one part in the beginning of *Catcher in the Rye* where Holden describes his roommate as a "secret slob"? I'm afraid that can describe me as well. My shoes are shined and my hair is clean. My desk is organized, things are collected promptly in files or stacked neatly in bins. However, the clasp on my bra is perilously close to breaking (I'm bustin' out!) and I just noticed there's a light smear of cream cheese on my monitor. (How the hell did I get cream cheese on my monitor?) My idea of cleaning the house is to pick up all the clutter and papers, remove the worst of the cat hair from the floors, and then sort of swipe at the bathroom with cleanser and a sponge. The apartment might look lovely, but there is secret filth. Nothing gross—if the cat vomited or the toilet got grungy I would certainly do something about it—but the filth is there. Lurking.

So in many ways LT and I are well-suited to live together. He is content to live among all manner of clutter, but when he cleans, it's bleach time. He's the floor mopper and the stove cleaner. He does the hard, germ-killing stuff. However, it's understandably not his favorite thing to do either. Which brings me long-windedly to the upshot of this discussion: I've gone over to the dark side. I've hired a "cleaning lady." I am yuppie scum.

It's not as bad as all that. Her name is Barbara, and right now she's only coming once a month, to get rid of the aforementioned secret filth. She is appallingly thorough. I had to stop her from cleaning the shelves of the refrigerator (which was not easy because there's a bit of a language barrier). She lives in the neighborhood and takes ESL classes at night. In the area of my brain labeled "Self-Justification," I like to think that everyone wins: she gets paid for a relatively easy once-a-month job, I get all those housecleaning things done that I really hate to do. Although, last time I was home when she came, and I must admit it's uncomfortably weird to be working at the computer and know that someone is cleaning your house. Hello, I'm Lady Mrs. Mimi Von Smartypants-Socialite, how do you do?

⟵ *July 27*

This weekend I attended a wedding in Madison, Wisconsin. Now there's a town that's just crawling with nonstop action. Oh wait! That's not action Madison is crawling with! It is actually crawling with *fleas* from all the *filthy goddamned hippies* all over the place! Man, I hate hippies. Overall, though, the Madison experience was tolerable. LT and I left Thursday night, drove through threatening thunderclouds although it never actually rained, checked into the Hilton at around 10 P.M., and hit the bar. We were staying on a "Club Floor," which as far as I could tell meant nothing whatsoever except some robes in the room and the inconvenience of having to use a key card for the elevator. The wedding was not until Friday evening, so we spent the morning in Madison visiting the tiny zoo, where we witnessed sexual intercourse between two lions. The lion humping took all of ten seconds. Afterward; the female lion split and the male lay on the ground exhausted for a bit, then got up on the largest rock in the enclosure and roared for a while, as if to say, "Yeah! Woooo! I'm the greatest! Wooooo! *Li-on! Li-on! Li-on!*"

Acting like dorks after getting some sweet loving? It's not just for humans anymore.

Also at the zoo, I got a Mold-a-Rama of an orange giraffe. If you don't know about Mold-a-Rama, I pity you. Mold-a-Rama is a souvenir machine that makes a useless plastic figurine, usually of an animal or a dinosaur. The best parts of Mold-a-Rama are (a) the name, (b) the swingin' 1960s font the name is printed in, (c) the fact that the whole Mold-a-Rama process takes place on display, through a plastic bubble, because there are very few opportunities for most of us to watch injection molding happen in person, and (d) the little mechanical spatula that scrapes your souvenir off the mold and drops it into the vending slot. I'm not sure why, but I find that mechanical spatula heartwarming.

Heartwarming! Mechanical! Spatula!

Sorry. After the zoo, we ditched the car and walked around State Street looking at all the goddamned hippies, had some satisfying Indonesian peanut sauce noodles and an incredibly unsatisfying cup of tea, and then went back to the hotel to dress for the wedding. I even wore real stockings and real shoes with heels. There's a first time for everything. The wedding was quite nice, except for the fact that it was outside, in a garden, and I quickly became covered with mosquito bites, and the minister's extended agricultural metaphor that started to drive me batty after a while. We plant the seed of love and harvest the crop of togetherness and reap the wheat of fidelity and fertilize with the manure of commitment and *blah blah what the hell are you talking about.* Luckily the whole thing was over fairly quickly and we could get on with the drinking and socializing. After the reception our group of dedicated lushes all met up again at the Hilton, where my dear husband quickly located the bar and bought most of it.

I came home to the most awesome mail. A friend of mine started doing marketing for a sock company (hey we all have to eat), and she sent me a giant padded envelope bulging with name-brand footwear. All kinds of sturdy, practical socks, and some weird ones too, including a pair that have the mysterious theme of "clambake" and are decorated with little pictures of lobsters and clams and corn on the cob and say *Clambake!* around the ankles. Hooray! (Coincidentally, there is an Elvis movie with the title *Clambake*, but it is too awful to sit through. Fast-forward to the part where Elvis sings the title song, which mostly goes like this: Clambake clambake, goin' to the clambake, clambake clambake gonna have a clambake. He dances around and tosses obviously fake lobsters into a pot on the beach. The minute I saw that I understood why Elvis had to spend so much time stoned out of his gourd.)

Thanks for listening. To sum up:
a. Heartwarming mechanical spatula.
b. Goddammed hippies.
c. Socks. Clambake. Elvis.

⟵ *July 30*

THREE REASONS WHY MY HUSBAND MIGHT BE A CYBORG

1. Barring extreme special occasions, he wears a uniform all the time. Black jeans and black T-shirts (in the summer) or black jeans and black sweaters (in the winter). He literally buys these things in bulk at Old Navy. He tends to refer to his pants as "pants-units" and to the shirts as "shirt-units."

2. He listens to one CD over and over and over again until I think I am going to have to run into the office and spray his computer with machine-gun fire. Then he will switch to another one and play that for a solid month. Lately he has switched from Johnny Cash to a French cha-cha-cha kick. This is not the musical taste of a human being.

3. He mows down civilians who get in his way, shoots the government's helicopters out of the air with his laser-beam eyes, and can grow a new head if his gets damaged. I think.

⟵ *August 6*

My parents moved into a house when I was around eight years old. Oh yeah, and they not only left me their for-warding address, they even brought me along. (You: Okay, smartass. Me: Listen, that joke had to be made.) It was my first experience having a backyard and I was all excited about it. There was even a crabapple tree that I liked to sit in and read, because that was my pointy-headed bespecta-cled anemic version of "playing outside." There was also a rope swing attached to a branch of a different tree, the kind of swing that is just a board with a hole through it and a single rope. Frankly the swing was a bit too close to the tree, which caused many cartoony accidents when the arc of your determined swinging would reach its peak and the whole thing would begin to collapse on itself, or a gust of wind would come along and turn you just enough so that you lost control and smashed into the tree trunk at high velocity. I received more than one faceful of bark that first summer, which may explain a few things and can we get a CT scan over here? I want to check my skull's integrity. Thanks.

So the whole backyard-wildlife thing was new to me. Consequently I was delighted when that same first summer there was an explosion in the toad population, which never was satisfactorily explained and I don't think ever happened since. I liked to catch the toads and hold their squishy fat bodies in my hands, and check out their really weird, almost catlike, eyes. We had an outdoor basement stairwell that was almost never used, and one day I set up a Toad Environment, with grass and sticks and water for them, and I caught around twenty toads and let them hop around their new home. Of course, being eight years old I then promptly forgot about the whole project, and the stairs were too tall for any of the toads to hop out, and so a month later when my dad had to go down those stairs for something he encountered the Toad Holocaust, the Toad Trail of Tears, the Toad Gulag, all these dead starved toads littering the stairwell. And there was no Amnesty International for toads, so all those toads just slowly starved to death, forgotten, and it was all my fault and I am still upset about it. I am the Forgetful Toad Stalin, who tortures out of absentmindedness rather than malice. Do the Toad Ghosts forgive me? Or will I be the sort of bug that is tasty to toads in my next life?

⟵ *August 8*

Back at work the inevitable afternoon doldrums and post–grilled cheese sleepiness was nicely interrupted by a phone call from LT. For reasons too dull and complex to explain here, he was standing by a duck pond and held out his cell phone so I could hear the ducks on my end. It made me laugh.

After work I was walking to a bar (shocking!) near the Chicago/Franklin El station. This is one of those weird El stations that has its exit a block away from its entrance, so that there are stairs at Superior and Franklin that are only for exiting, and in fact, just so you don't get confused, there is a STOP! NO ENTRY! sticker on each stair riser. As I walk by

I see this artsy-looking hipster dude come out of one of the galleries. I guess noticing your environment, including giant STOP! NO ENTRY! signs, is not part of the artsy hipster dude schtick, because he starts to head up those well-labeled stairs. Helpfully, and with a very pleasant tone, I say, "You can't go up that way," and *immediately* this guy, still climbing, yells down, "Go to hell." Go to hell? I should go to hell? Oh my goodness. This is rather a strong comment to make to someone who is merely trying to give you a time-saving hint. I finished crossing the street, so that I could have a full view of the stairs, and turned around and watched this guy get to the top, discover that indeed that turnstile only works one way, and start to walk back down. Then I waved and called out (still helpfully, still with a very pleasant tone), "Have a nice day!"

←—*August 10*

LT and I had friends over for dinner and after the guests had left I was all wide-awake, and wanted to finish my wine and answer some e-mail. Somehow through a combination of my own tipsy impulsivity and Hotmail's tiny-font overly-clickable home page I ended up entering the "chat" section, something I had never done before. What the hell, I thought. Let's see what this is all about.

Well, *mystery solved*. Now I know precisely what chat rooms are all about. They are all about annoying the shit out of me. The minute my virtual self virtually showed up in the virtual room I started getting about eight messages a minute, mostly of the ever-obnoxious "A/S/L?" variety. Also a fair number from robots, inviting me to go watch them masturbate on their webcams (if they were true robots instead of just spammified chat bots from porn sites I might be intrigued because that whole human-mechanical sex thing would be kind of futuristic and cool. But alas.) I quickly realized this chat room scene was not at all for me, but not before having the following pure-comedy-gold exchange (all terrible spelling has been preserved, but screennames have been slightly changed to protect the hot and the male).

HottMale34: Hello

mimismartypants: Hello hot male.

mImismartypants: Why did you name yourself hot male?

mimismartypants: That is kind of odd.

mimismartypants: It's like you are insisting you are hot and you are male, both of which should be self-evident.

HottMale34: Thats all i was able to come up with

mimismartypants: How sad. Are "hot" and "male" really your only attributes?

mimismartypants: An impoverished existence, to be sure.

HottMale34: u talk to much

mimismartypants: A subjective verdict, and an odd complaint to voice in a "chat" room, but I'll give it to you. "Verbose" is one of my attributes.

HottMale34: stick a big dick in that big mouth

mimismartypants: From whence, this big dick?

HottMale34: if i stick my big dick in your mouth would u stop talking?

mimismartypants: It's kind of a moot point, isn't it? We are each free to leave this conversation at any time, and there is no big dick in evidence.

HottMale34: you're so dumb

mimismartypants: As a sack of hammers!

HottMale34: bye

mimismartypants: Goodbye, sir!

←*August 10*

I wish I could quit having dual-consciousness in dreams. For instance, last night I fell quickly asleep at around 10:30 after drinking a bunch of wine with dinner and then snuggling under a blanket with LT while we watched some of those Discovery Channel forensic shows, the ones that teach you *never to kill anybody* because one lousy hair or fragment of skull will send you to jail forever. I like these programs because they are all science-worshipping, which is sexy, and there is one that is narrated by the *Frontline* guy, which is sexier. If I was married to that guy I'd make him read the paper to me every night. Anyway, I soon got sleepy and we went to bed, and my brain, lulled into snuggly domesticity by the dinner and the wine and the television, started to dream this dream where I was tidying up our bookshelves. The bookshelves had a lot more than just books on them, there were hairbrushes and toys and old plates of leftover cookies and candy from Christmas. I was tidying them up in preparation for a houseguest, who was a space alien. "Wait a minute," I told myself (still dreaming). "You cannot just randomly throw in a space alien whenever you think your dream is getting too cozy and boring." Then (*still* dreaming), I told myself to butt out, I wasn't just randomly throwing it in there, this dream would have continuity soon enough, just give me a chance to tie all the loose ends together. This is not the first time my dreams have featured a whole lot of narrative interruption and a postmodern undermining of authorial intention, and I worry that if this keeps up I will never have action-packed narrative dreams again but instead all my dreams will feature a bunch of irritating fragments of "self" sitting around and arguing about the literary merit of the dream. Help me.

◄— *August 14*

Whenever I get . . . not depressed exactly, but moody and introspective, I have a very particular set of symptoms. The weirdest thing is what happens to my vision. I get fascinated by minute things. The grain patterns in wood. The quality of light as it slides around and drips off all the metal surfaces in the subway car, around sunset. The twisty patterns of black tree branches. Even my own pale, scratched-up hand poking out of my coat sleeve. When I'm happy I attend more to the macro view, on grayer days it's the tiny things that seem incredibly important.

Come to think of it, all my favorite toys as a child had the same sort of hypnotic, trance-inducing quality. I used to like to ride my tricycle in a circle, and I was addicted to this wonderful thing called a Lemon Twist. It was a loop of rubber that fit around your ankle, with a short piece of rubber off of that and a plastic lemon (why a lemon?) at the end that had some sort of pebbles or other noisemakers inside. You'd skip over the lemon and get a rhythm going. I could do that for hours. And let's not forget Sit and Spin, Spirograph, the little magnetic wheel on two tracks that went up and down as you squeezed it, and Lite-Brite, which for me was always less about the artistic process than it was about the incredibly satisfying thunk of those pegs as they pushed through the black paper.

Okay, now I feel the need to spin around in my office chair until that same sort of dizzy transcendence is achieved.

I keep forgetting to mention that tomorrow I take off for NYC, where I will no doubt, immediately upon stepping out of the cab from LaGuardia, get hooked on smack and end up gyrating disinterestedly around a pole, track marks on my skinny shanks and a thousand-yard stare shining out of my purple-rimmed eyes, sweaty furtive men waving fistfuls of slightly damp singles toward my sequined bikini'd ass. Okay, not really. I'm going to hang out with my friend, drink a lot of tea, and smell big-city smells other than those available in Chicago. I also plan to look at some art while I'm there. Hey, I'm a cultured girl. When I have a spare moment there's nothing I like better than to get out a batch of art and look at it.

⟵ *August 17*

Ah, New York. I'm all yours, New York. You had me at "I'm going to shove that fucking backpack up your ass." Which is what some stereotyped Latina girl (achingly tight ponytail, cleavage shirt with gold name necklace, black lipliner) announced as her intent, when I bumped into her a tiny bit on the street on my first full day in the city. I sound like I'm being sarcastic but I'm not: I love New York, and if I were a millionaire I'd be buying a second apartment there. I had a fabulous time. That particular tightly wound senorita did not spoil things one bit (and she also did not shove my backpack up my ass, thank god).

I'm still undecided as to whether to let New York details sort of dribble out (eeww, gross) or to do a straight summing-up of the trip. Friday my hostess had to go to work so I spent the day at MoMA and some art galleries, went to Gotham Book Mart and found the very translation of *The Gambler* (the Dostoyevsky book, not the Kenny Rogers song) I had been looking for, and had a most excellent cookie and cup of tea at a deserted coffee shop, where they didn't squawk at all about how long I stayed reading and typing and getting all overcaffeinated. Dinner, drinking, and so forth then ensued. (What else is new, right?)

Saturday my friend and I shopped all over SoHo and the Lower East Side: the Strand (god I love the Strand. So! Many! Books! Okay, that's enough, if I think about it too much I get a case of the vapors), sparkly girly barrettes and things, etc. We ate lunch at a place that serves only grilled cheese and then drank red wine in the middle of the afternoon at Lotus Bar (so decadent). Again with the late-night dinner and the drinks, including beers at a completely unmarked basement bar (you just have to be "in the know," and because I am an incredible dork that made me feel briefly cool). It was some regular's birthday, balloons and cake everywhere, and we had the tipsy munchies and so helped ourselves despite not being at all entitled to do so. I don't think anyone noticed. Happy birthday Allison, whoever you are.

Sunday I was still feeling like an Art Whore so I went to the Armory Show while she ran errands. Some things were very good, some things were pretentious drivel, but overall I was very impressed with most of what I saw. One of the prettiest (if not the most earth-shattering) pieces was a quilt that someone had made by sewing found drug baggies together (the little ones that crack comes in). They were all different colors and patterns and it was just a nice artsy-craftsy effect. *Drug bag quilts are precious family heirlooms to be treasured. Make one for your future grandchildren.*

That evening we went to an "open mic," a so-called genre that normally induces immediate projectile vomiting in me, because why in the name of all that is true and good would you subject yourself to bad poetry and boring acoustic folk songs about vaginas? However, this open mic rocked the house, and that wasn't just the (openly smoked in the performance space) marijuana talking. Each slot was only six minutes long, so while not everything was good, even the worst thing wouldn't hurt you too badly. There was a woman who did a striptease while performing Nina's climactic monologue from *The Seagull*, a socialist puppet show in verse about an evil landlord (much more entertaining than it sounds), a song about Lou Reed's cock, some creative stand-up (again, normally something I consider to be a half step above mime in the Art Forms That Suck category), and a question-and-answer session titled "Ask an Ex-Mormon." It was a very fun night, although I stayed up too late and felt tired and gritty on the plane. In fact I fell into this weird half-sleep in flight (during the whole nap I was aware that I had my mouth a bit open, and it bothered me in a self-conscious way, but I felt sort of paralyzed and unable to do anything about it). I had a dream that I was having sex with an unknown person, right there on the floor of the plane, and the flight attendant asked us to please move to the exit row so we wouldn't block the aisle and they could have the beverage service. I think she even pointed out in the safety demonstration that the exit row was the safest place to have sex in the event of an emergency.

━━ *August 18*

I had gone a fairly long time without public transportation crazies, but my streak was broken this morning. A fairly normal-looking guy (clean, shaven, no tinfoil hat) sat next to me on the El and then kept up a running dialogue with himself, all angry-like, and then he started to gesture a lot, and I tried to ignore this because, as you know, the golden rule of city life is *never provoke the crazy*. I was trying to just be cool about the violation of my personal space, and even after his gestures actually made contact with my arm I still tried to be cool, but then the second time this happened I had had enough so I loudly said, *"Do not touch me."* The really funny thing is that he gave *me* a weird look and got up and moved.

Pretend you are me. Because it is warm, and because you have a meeting of some importance today, you decided to wear your Purple Dress. Your Purple Dress is on the grown-up side, and requires proper stockings rather than schoolgirl tights. Of course, there is some universal karmic rule that says that all will be fine when you put on the proper stockings at home. Look at me, you will think, I am a grown-up lady with proper stockings. Then you will get to work and immediately acquire a huge run in said grown-up stockings, and you will say, "Oh *fuck me*" quite loudly in your office (today is all about the outbursts, I guess) and probably alienate the extremely Christian coworker in the office next to you. You will briefly consider shredding the stockings further, deliberately, and rocking a sort of Nina Hagen/Siouxsie Sioux/Cyndi Lauper nihilist punk look, but that would defeat the purpose of the Purple Dress. So off you go, first thing in the morning, even before the tea, to purchase more leg coverings. White Hen will turn out only to carry queen-sized stockings, and since you are more of a princess or lady-in-waiting or scullery maid size, you will have to walk all the way to Walgreens. There you will purchase not the expensive-but-worth-it-for-the-sensual-payoff fake-silk brand that you prefer, but a brand that promises to "gently hug your legs to create an incredibly vibrant tingly feeling that goes nonstop throughout your busy day." You will wonder how they knew your day was going to be busy. How do they know you are not some throwback June Cleaver lady, putting on a dress and pearls just to down a bunch of amphetamine diet pills and vacuum really fast? You will also decide that, if you wanted an "incredibly vibrant tingly feeling," in your legs or elsewhere (ahem), you would not fuck around with a pair of stockings but go right to the battery-operated source. As it were.

← *August 19*

On my lunchtime jaunt out to get food I ran into these Greenpeace people. I hate being interrupted on my lunchtime jaunts, but I ended up pledging ten bucks a month because the Greenpeace Girl was this extremely cute husky-voiced soccer-playing lesbotronic chick with an arm tattoo of an ice cream cone. I am a *sucker* with a capital *suck*. Ah well, I guess Greenpeace is a good cause and I can certainly swing ten bucks a month. I would like Greenpeace better if they weren't all such hippies, though, since hippies in general make me angry. I have been known to fly into a psychotic smashy-smashy rage at the smell of patchouli or the sight of a hemp necklace or the sound of some obnoxious Phish-style guitar-noodle wankery. (Okay, let's finish this: or the feel of scratchy poncho fabric or the taste of something from the Moosewood cookbook. Whew.) Even worse then regular hippies are the faux hippies, the thick-necked frat-boy jocks who have just discovered marijuana and the Dave Matthews Band and they get themselves some sort of Guatemalan anorak and pretend like they are poor before heading off to business school. LT and I were visiting Boston once, and there was this kid in Harvard Square panhandling (wearing expensive shoes, of course, and probably going to go home to a four-bedroom house in Newton later that night), and as we passed the kid said, "Kick a hippie, fifty cents." It was tempting, but LT convinced me that it would be better not to get involved.

*← **August 24***

My weekend went like this: nap; nap; feel guilty about the vast reserves of domestic energy LT is expending (doing laundry, grocery shopping); decide not to feel guilty because I work hard all week, dammit; wonder if I am becoming some sort of suburban-dad stereotype, wanting nothing more than to drink beer and watch football on the weekends; cook a yummy dinner, or rather cook up various side dishes while LT does most of the work; have my sister over; kick her ass in Scrabble; spend some tea-drinking time with people I like; chase down the tea with beer later that afternoon, which I believe is known in drug circles as a "speedball" and is how that guy from Alice in Chains died. Kind of. Same idea, anyway.

It looks like I am becoming the culture liaison to my upper management at work. Besides teaching everybody what "huffing" is (it came up in an article), I recently had to give a detailed and somewhat bizarre explanation when we had several e-mails going back and forth on a certain topic, and to distinguish between the original topic and the updated, new information on the topic I titled my first e-mail something like "Topic" and the second one "Topic 2: Electric Boogaloo." Then I had to put up with a third round of e-mails about what the heck I meant by that. And you just try explaining to your boss that there once was a movie called *Breakin'* and that its sequel, inexplicably, was called *Breakin' 2: Electric Boogaloo*. Then try explaining that ever since that particular point in the twentieth century, "Electric Boogaloo" has seemed like a really appropriate subtitle for just about anything. Next, move on to explaining that you were making a joke, albeit a really lame one, and can we all just move on if you promise never, ever, to wig out like that again in a business setting? Close your office door and pull out your secret flask of Jim Beam. Lather, rinse, repeat.

— August 27

I am a freak. Someone has been slipping some sort of Lust Elixir in my tea, I think, because I am all wiggly and squirmy like a wiggly squirmy mink. Yesterday morning before I even went to my office I had to go drop something off on another floor, and I was all alone in the elevator with its shiny mirrored interior, so I spent the entire ride striking suggestive poses like I was a backup singer for Prince or something. Except with no fingerless lace gloves, and no similarly big-haired severe-makeup girl hanging over my shoulder and helping me play the synthesizer. Do you remember all those Prince girls? Apollonia and Vanity and all those other funny-named people? What do you think they are doing right now?

Anyway, I hope this lustful squirmy mood passes quickly, because it will not do to be all riled up like this every day at work, because sometimes I have to use terms like "dangling modifier" or "endoscopic retrograde cholangiopancreatography," or I have to figure out how to cite the *Congressional Record,* and these are all very sexy things that could push me over the edge if that lustful squirmy mood is still around. Next thing you know I am dirty-dancing on top of my desk with office supplies for props.

The only action I saw at work yesterday, though, was from a decidedly nonhuman entity. I am calmly doing my thing in Microsoft Word and suddenly, from nowhere, Clippy appears, hangs around for a while blinking his big bedroom eyes, and then disappears. I swear I touched nothing, and I certainly had not asked for "help." Clippy is flirting with me. Clippy says please baby please. Clippy says okay baby, trust me, just touch it a little bit, please. Clippy says, "It looks like you are getting naked. Would you like help getting naked?" And Mimi is traumatized for weeks by nightmares of humping Microsoft's animated paper clip.

◄── *August 28*

I can take my lunch hour whenever I want. It says so right in the employee handbook. So when you send me an e-mail at 11:52, requesting an "urgent" meeting in your office at noon, and I do not get the e-mail or make the meeting because *I am at lunch,* please do not barge into my office right as I return, and snarkily say, "Well, we met without you" and proceed to detail the nonemergency. Yes, you did meet without me because *I was not here.* Please put a radio collar or ear tag on me if it is that crucial that I be a hundred percent reachable at all times, or better yet why don't you just ban lunch altogether and let me shrivel up like a Dickens waif.

Also, in my office there has been a major crackdown on electric teakettles, in the form of a sternly worded memo that emphasized how "very dangerous" these puny-wattage water boilers are, and how they pose a "substantial threat" (I really am quoting—it is all like *Orange alert someone is making tea!*) to the entire building, and how if anyone is found making tea at his or her desk instead of trekking downstairs to the cafeteria and paying high prices for inferior tea and icky coffee-residue hot water, that person's electric teakettle will be "immediately confiscated." Your freedom fighter correspondent, Mimi Smartypants, casts a heroic shadow in the romantic manner of the French Resistance as she crouches behind her closed office door and clandestinely boils water for her afternoon Earl Grey. Hooray *pour le thé*! They'll never take me alive!

◄—*August 29*

I am having a lot of trouble staying on task today. At work this morning I did a Big Difficult Thing, and then I decided to reward myself for accomplishing the BDT with a little bit of slacktime, and the next thing you know an hour and a half has gone by. My slacktime was nothing special either, nothing stylish like sneaking out to a bar or committing white-collar crimes. A little bit of e-mail, a little bit of staring out the window, a little bit of making a puppet out of a Styrofoam coffee cup, paper clips, and a straw, and then decorating the puppet with markers, and then having the puppet perform Bikini Kill's "New Radio," and it seems I am suddenly the queen of wasting time. Did that puppet ever rock out too; you should have seen her. I named her Styrrrofoamalina.

⸺ *September 1*

When I finally stopped futzing around and left the house this morning, I was witness to a whole bunch of little brown birds cheeping and screaming and fluttering all over each other in a little brown bird riot. I have seen birdy skirmishes before, but this was extreme Bird Fight Tonight. If we may extrapolate for a moment from birds to people, this was no emo-boy striped-sweater fight where they push each other a little and then their friends hold them back, and they struggle a tiny bit but they are both secretly relieved. No, this was a skinny mulleted redneck missing-key-teeth sixteen-Pabst-Blue-Ribbons fight, where this 105-pound dude just gets in there and won't stop, even after it is clear the other guy is unconscious. This was a Chickadee Beatdown. I had never seen anything like it: a mass of sparrows or wrens or whatever the fuck (no bird-watcher, I) all a-wrassling on the ground.

After that amazing spectacle, my bird-noticing-feelers must have been tuned to an extra-high frequency, because while I waited for the bus I watched this really weird-looking yellow-beaked bird, very small and dark but with giant feet, eat a french fry twice as long as his body. He did not peck at it like a regular bird but picked the fry up, somehow got it vertical, and made it disappear down his gullet like a sword-swallower. Then the bird gave me a threatening look. Really. Birds kind of give me the heebie-jeebies in general, despite the fact that my very first pet, Mr. Tweeters (I never did know his first name) was a parakeet. So I was a little twitchy on the bus, and my surreal commuting experience (*Where did that bird put that giant french fry?*) was not helped any by a field trip of about ten mentally challenged adults, from the area group home, who were shepherded onto the bus at Clark Street. I know it is not politically correct to be freaked out by the mentally challenged but sometimes it is hard to control your freaked-outedness, particularly if you had just watched some crazy bird defy the laws of anatomy and then glare at you with its beady bird eyes.

⟵ September 4

I had to go on a business trip recently, to Pittsburgh, and it is really too boring to even mention. Except for, you know, all those little details that I feel compelled to mention.

AIRPORT STUFF

Signs in the arrivals area of O'Hare Airport mention "dwell time." Areas in which you cannot linger say, NO DWELL TIME. Gather ye rosebuds while ye may! Carpe diem! No dwell time!

Pittsburgh Airport seems more overtly security-conscious than O'Hare. I had to take off my shoes, my messenger bag was sent through X-ray several times, and ultimately the flirtatious and jocular airport security guy searched my bag with dedicated thoroughness, including going through my wallet ("Want to loan me ten bucks?"), opening and *smelling* my bag of dried fruit ("Healthy snacks, cool!"), and commenting on my technical gadgets ("Is that a Handspring?"). Someone should tell him that macking on girls who are on their way *out* of town is not terribly productive. Finally he pulled out my keys, which are attached to a small plastic dinosaur key ring. "Ah, here's the trouble," he said. "T. Rex is a ferocious carnivore! You can't bring this creature on an airplane!" Ha ha. Oh Airport Security Guy, you crack me up. Sort of.

Also witnessed at security was a cute small boy with a death grip on a stuffed dog. The parentals were trying to convince him to put it through the X-ray machine, putting a positive spin on the idea: Look! Growly will get to go on a fun ride on this conveyer belt! Won't that be great? However, the kid was having none of it, not crying yet but really really close, and the airport security guys were kind of clustered around with their arms folded, exchanging wry indulgent smiles but also giving the impression that they would not be above taking Growly for that X-ray ride by force, if necessary.

⟵ *September 5*

Recently I heard a news story about a hiker who was trapped under a boulder and ended up cutting off his own arm. To me, this story illustrates several things that I have been saying for years. Never, ever, go out into nature. What does Mother Nature want from us? The answer is obvious: She Wants Our Limbs. For instance: frostbite. Giant crushing boulders. Wolverines that can rip off an arm with one clamp of their wolverine jaws. Muskrats that first incapacitate you with a tendon-severing ankle bite, then nibble and nibble until your leg is entirely gone. Go ahead, scream your lungs out during your Nibbling Ordeal, do you think Mother Nature cares? She is all like, Listen mother-fucker, what exact part of "red in tooth and claw" don't you understand? Don't come to me singing your sad limb-losing song. You were warned.

Let me, Mimi Smartypants, be your Johnnie Cochran for one moment: If It Ain't Concrete, You Must Retreat. After this news story, I am hesitant to walk in the damn park. I am sticking to the city sidewalks and to the great indoors, or, if I have to walk in nature for any reason, I am considering wearing a straitjacket because it keeps the limbs nice and enclosed and away from dangers. Or maybe a giant hamster ball or John-Travolta-Boy-in-the-Plastic-Bubble contraption. I only have four limbs, and I need them all, and even though being known as That Person Who Severed His or Her Own Arm with a Pocketknife pretty much assures you of buckets and buckets of bad-ass cred until the end of time (can you imagine?), I'd rather not, thank you. *No nature no hiking no camping none of that foolishness. No.*

Of course this Arm-Severing Guy was all over the tele-vision, and, desperate for related stories so as not to let the arm-severing excitement die down for even one freaking minute, CNN spent some time this morning telling the story of *another* guy who went hiking and ended up hav-ing to cut something off. This guy had a boulder (see, the boulders have it in for us *I'm telling you*) fall on his leg, and after being unable to free himself he ended up cutting his leg off below the knee with a pocketknife and then some-how driving to the next town for help. Important differ-ence, though: whereas Arm-Severing Guy was trapped for

six days, this guy apparently waited only *one day*. Okay. He
said that there was a snowstorm coming, and that his leg
really hurt, and so on, but still: don't you wait a little
longer than one day? I know that you can never really
predict what you would do in a crisis, but I feel fairly comfortable in predicting that I would work on screaming for
at least two solid days before I even started thinking about
holding a do-it-yourself amputation party. I worry a bit
about this one-day guy. Maybe if the pizza is a half-hour
late he is already starting to toss names into a hat to decide
who gets eaten. You lock your keys in the car and he
smashes in the window immediately rather than try any
coat hanger or slim jim business. I don't know, maybe he
is right, and it was his only option, but still. One day of
trapped.

September 8

There are way too many sitcoms and other programs
where the characters work "in publishing," and usually it is
some sort of glamour thing like fashion or architecture or a
big hard-hitting newsweekly. Oh, and also they don't seem
to work too terribly hard, and have big open-plan offices
where people can gather to trade witticisms and such. I
know that is just a function of the way that shit needs to be
staged and videotaped, but it still rankles a bit, because *I*
work in publishing, and we are mostly freaked-out moles
stuck typing in offices and cubicles, and I am one of the few
purveyors of any witticisms at all in my office, which gives
you an idea of how hard up this place must be for witti-

cisms. Also, those glamour jobs at name-brand magazines are just about impossible to come by, being mostly reserved for either nepotism purposes or trust-fund babies who can afford a year or two of an unpaid internship, and the people I know professionally usually work on scientific or technical journals, or in various industry throwaways about computers or travel, or on in-flight magazines, or at hard-to-mention-socially publishing houses—like the acquaintance of mine who got a job at a publisher of third- or fourth-tier "men's magazines." One of the titles in their catalog was something called *Forced Enema*. Personally I would have taken great pride in being tapped as the editor of *Forced Enema* but he did not.

━ *September 10*

ONE HUNDRED PENNIES

Last night Sophie and I held a reprise of dollar-beer Tuesday at the Long Room. *Dollar. Beer. One dollar.* Both Schlitz and PBR are available at this lovely, lovely price on Tuesdays, and while both are bad beers I suggest you go for the Schlitz. At least Schlitz is made with clean water, whereas in my opinion Pabst is made with detox sweat. I have visited the Pabst brewery (on my honeymoon no less!), and I did not see any junkies bent over perspiration-collection vats while they went through agonizing withdrawal, but maybe they were in the back. Anyway, if you are a thrifty sort, not a beer snob, and are in Chicago on a Tuesday, I have to recommend the Long Room. Except for the gaggle of boys near us who were loudly comparing puke stories. You guys can stay home.

Afterward, my cabdriver complained about going back up to Devon since he had just been there. Shout-out to Chicago's taximen: the minute you bitch about my destination, the tip starts dwindling. I missed the part where I am supposed to care that you do not feel like going to the airport or downtown or whatever. Last night's guy also tried to tell me that my neighborhood was "dangerous" (not true), and that "they will slash your tires there." He would not elaborate on who "they" were when I asked. I came home, drank some water, and fell into sweet Schlitzy slumber very quickly. Sleep featured a dream where I was standing on a down escalator in Woodfield Mall, out in the suburbs, with a large telepathic dog, and I was explaining to him how much I hate Robert's Rules. "It's a stupid goddamn system," I told the dog. "It's like metric. Maybe it would be nice if everyone used it, but no one really knows how and we just *don't*, so give up the dream already." The dog told me, in his mind, that he thought I was absolutely right, and did I remember where we parked? (Note: I really do think Robert's Rules are kind of stupid. Every time I attend a meeting where they are half-assedly used, people end up spending a lot of time discussing the rules themselves rather than actually getting to the point. However, I have never shared my viewpoint on this with a telepathic dog.)

⟵ *September 13*

For months and months now, LT has been answering certain phone calls (me, friends, telemarketers) with a thick mysterious accent (vaguely Arabic, vaguely Eastern European, vaguely *Simpsons* klav kalash guy) and the words, "Hello, Monkey Store!" See, Monkey Store Guy runs a monkey store. He sells monkeys. In broken English, he offers, "All kinds monkey. Spider monkey, rhesus monkey. You want monkey? No? Then why you call Monkey Store?" I have started to play along when I call, either pretending to be a Monkey Store customer with an equally mysterious accent, the owner of a rival monkey store ("Listen! My monkeys better, cheaper! We crush you! Crush! You!"), or a representative from the health department. This last exchange was particularly hilarious (to us):

(ring)
LT: *Hello! Monkey Store!*
Me: Hello, I'm calling from the Board of Health. Is this the proprietor?
(long pause)
LT: *No Monkey Store! Goodbye!*

⟵ *September 16*

I think I may be getting crazier.

For one thing, I am talking to myself a lot more. (Of course, one could argue that this very diary is the ultimate expression of "talking to myself," in which case I have been extra super hypercrazy for a while now.)

LT was out at his Chinese class last night and I decided to go to bed early. Only once I got there, I realized I was not terribly sleepy, and I decided to, um, spend a little quality time with myself. (Yes, even though it makes the baby Jesus cry. What can I say, The Girl Can't Help It.) When I was finished, for some inexplicable reason I said, *out loud*, to no one, "Thank you very much, ladies and gentlemen! Good night!"

Also, my more-or-less-constant low-level obsessive-compulsive disorder has flared up recently. Not to any critical level where I have trouble leaving the house due to my numerologically based rituals. However, this morning I alphabetized all the possible breakfast choices, and then somehow my usual routine for choosing between options (I won't go into it here, but it is based on the date) was not working for me, so I used an online random number generator to help me make the decision to have an English muffin. People. Seriously. I need to be kicked in the head. A fucking *random number generator* was the only way I could quit doddering and dithering between insignificant choices and pick a breakfast food. Although on some level I think this is rather resourceful of me. I came up with a definitive, authoritative, Web-based way to settle my stuck-brain OCD problem rather than just succumbing to panic, as I might have ten years ago. (Yeah sure. I will just keep telling myself that.)

← *September 17*

WHAT RULES AND WHAT SUCKS (IN THE WORKPLACE)

My new work chair: rules! My new chair is so very adjustable that one could easily spend a good two hours of one's morning adjusting it, which is precisely what I did today. The arms go in and out and up and down, there is some sort of lumbar (gosh that word sounds dirty to me) support knob that sends a bulge of comfort up or down your spinal column (rrrrowwrr!), and the seat can tilt all sorts of crazy ways like you are playing one of those flight-simulator arcade games. Plus the seat is *extra super wide!* There is so much room, you could come sit in the chair with me! Really! Or I could gain fifty pounds in the ass location and still keep my job! Okay, I have to stop, I am getting too excited.

The rest of work: sucks! I am losing yet another employee! I thought there was supposed to be a recession or something! Goddammit, be recessed! I suppose it is my fault for hiring these young talented go-getters, and honestly I am not one of those bosses who takes it all personally when someone leaves. Everyone has to forge his or her own path, fly little birdie be free, etc. But it sucks for me because it means lots of cruddy HR paperwork, lots of extra tasks while we are down a person, and lots of self-consciousness and cold sweats while I play the interviewing game again. And it sucks for this diary, because I will probably talk about the process here, and then part of my brain will be thinking, *Same old same old shut up*, another part of my brain will be thinking, *Don't yell at me okay I can write what I want*, and a third part will think, *time for a beer where did you put the bottle opener*.

━ *September 18*

HERE IS WHAT HAPPENS WITH TOO MUCH TEA

1. Why is there no astronaut porn?

2. There should be astronaut porn!

3. Is NASA blocking the production of astronaut porn? Fuck NASA! America is a free country, where we can freely make astronaut porn!

4. I mean, think about it! The whole uniform thing! Like cops! Or auto mechanics! Or soldiers! Those archetypes have their own porn niche, so why not astronauts?

5. And the "squeaky clean virginal military type/scientist is defiled with hot man-on-man action" thing!

6. In Space, No One Can Hear You Ream!

7. Boldly Going Where No Man Has Gone Before!

8. Houston, We Have a Problem. A Sexy Problem!

9. And of course the obvious, "Ass-tronauts"!

10. Words like "thrust"! "Boost"! "O-rings"! "Tang"!

11. Zero-gravity cumshots and such would be strangely beautiful!

12. There are lots of female astronauts now, so even heterosexuals can get in on the action!

13. Maybe even First Gangbang in Space! Heck why not!

14. Swarthy Russian cosmonauts!

September 20

Lunchtime conversation at CVS, purveyor of cheap toiletries: my greeting card, bottle of vitamin B-complex, box of tampons, Altoids Cinnamon Strips, and large bottle of water came to twenty-one dollars exactly.

Me: Wow, cool.

CVS Girl: What?

Me: No, uh, nothing. Just that it's unusual for a total to be a round number like that, with no change.

CVS Girl: Twenty-one dollars? That ain't a round number.

Me: Well, it's twenty-one dollars exactly, right? That's the total.

CVS Girl (who by this time has already taken my twenty-one dollars and now is just staring at me)**:** A round number is something like twenty dollars. Twenty-*one* dollars is what you had.

Me: Yeah, but . . . okay, never mind.

CVS Girl: Have a good day.

Me: You too.

September 23

I had a very terrible bus ride home.

a. On the bus was my least favorite crazy person, the guy who screams often and with no warning and pounds on the bus window with his fist.

b. On the bus it felt like the air conditioning and the heat were on simultaneously.

c. On the bus was a weird smell, like a fire in a candy factory.

d. On the bus I had to witness this slack-jawed woman *shake* and *pinch* her toddler awake, saying, "Wake up! Wake up! Wake up now!" for god knows what reason, I guess so that she wouldn't have to exert her lazy ass to carry this extremely small child off the bus.

I feel sorry for all children, and not just the ones who are pinched and shaken for doing something age-appropriate like falling asleep on the bus. I would never say I had an unhappy childhood, because I had nothing to be unhappy about, but I was unhappy just plain being a kid, and I never looked forward to the next grade or birthday or going to high school or college. (Although in retrospect I should have been looking forward to college, because I ended up very much enjoying the bastion of pseudo-adulthood it is. Like playing with the other kids in a big, safe, intellectual sandbox. With liquor.) I just wanted the childness and the powerlessness to be over with *now*. I wanted to be an adult. Being an adult is exponentially preferable to being a kid. So now I have this weird intense empathy for babies and children and teenagers. Even when I witness them in public being horrible, I just want to telepathically say, "I know. This sucks. I'm sorry you have to be a kid. I'm sorry that TV talks down to you and no one understands and everything you need is stored on high shelves. Just try and wait it out."

⟵ *September 29*

Okay, so I had a little cold. So I stay home from work for one day, but then I go back, because just a little sore throat isn't anything to baby oneself over, right? And then Iris calls me on Friday, and she's ever so much fun, so me and my tiny insignificant sore throat go over to her house, and we sit on the back porch and drink cheap ice-cold pinot blanc and talk and talk and talk, and then we go to the Pontiac Café (which is horrible, by the way: decent bruschetta but just about the worst of halter-topped and baseball-capped jerks all gathered in one place) and drink Bass and talk and talk, and then we go pick up Kat, and then we walk to Lemmings and talk and talk and drink more beer and talk and talk, and sometime around midnight I'm getting a little throaty, I'm getting a little June Allyson/Lauren Bacall; and there's some weird guy who insists on addressing me as "kitten," but that's another story; and there's another weird guy who quotes Billy Joel lyrics at me in a misguided attempt at flirting, but that's yet another, even sadder, story; and by 2 A.M. I'm getting a weird adolescent-boy break in my voice; and I go home and go to sleep and the next morning I cannot talk at all.

This is new to me. I have not been able to speak above a whisper since Saturday morning. Today I went back to work, and I had to put a sign up on my office door asking people to communicate with me through e-mail only, and I had to have someone else record a voice mail message on my phone asking authors and remote editors to please e-mail me instead, and when I went to buy a sandwich at lunch I had to write my order out on an index card like a sad little Mute Girl. We had to cancel dinner plans we had for tonight (LT called and gave the other couple the option of coming anyway, but they said, "No point in hanging with Mimi if you don't get the benefit of her witty banter," which in a way makes me sad that the Fun of Me is all wrapped up in words, but in another way makes me pleased that I am not merely a decorative bibelot).

Anyway. This is getting old. It was briefly fun to practice my mime/charades skills, and LT has had fun speaking "for" me like a ventriloquist, but now it is getting old. Under duress, I went to the doctor today, and it is just as I thought: complete voice rest, hot liquids, and aspirin. Not rock and roll screaming, sweet cool beer, and barbiturates. Sigh.

← *September 30*

MUSINGS ON THE ALPHABET

When I was little my favorite letters were ones that had their own completely enclosed spaces: A, B, D, O, P, Q, R. I wanted to get inside that space and sit there. To be inside the O! Would be O so nice! The A would be like an attic room, and with the B you get a two-story house. When I learned about lowercase letters I was vaguely troubled that some letters lost their safehouses (like r) but happy that more had gained them (e and g).

I don't remember not knowing how to read. I learned on my own, at some point, definitely by around three years old at the latest. Sometimes I look at pages of dense foreign text to try and taste the soup of pure alphabet (what a great Campbell's spinoff that would be—vegetable broth with *noodle-shaped glyphs* or *glyph-shaped noodles, take your pick*). Unfortunately, my brain always starts picking out words I know in that language, or zooms to the one English word, or finds some root that is enough like another root so that I am back to puzzling out meaning. Not that I really want to forget how to read (god, what a nightmare), I just want to leave words behind temporarily and spend a little quality time with the alphabet, which is not always easy to do, what with both of us being so busy and all.

Particularly with nouns, I often try to enjoy the shape of a word just as a shape, but meaning comes creeping in. (Stupid meaning, always creeping in.) Which came first, the shape or the meaning? The double oo in "book" like a pair of reading glasses. Or even the word "cunt," which sounds so ugly but looks so nice, with those first three rounded, cupped letters with the openings to the side, up, and down. It looks like a series of little caves next to a tree.

You can have words without an alphabet (pictograms, hieroglyphics, Chinese) but if you have an alphabet words will inevitably follow.

A particularly dorky period of my life found me writing in my journal in a fake "code" that was just English written in Greek letters. Now when I write notes to myself I often use a made-up personal shorthand where I leave out all the vowels. Sometimes I forget what I was driving at and then I have to play a mental version of *Wheel of Fortune* to figure it out.

←*October 1*

I had to go to a work meeting today, led by someone who is a Large Cheese in the company. I was very impressed with the high-quality bullshit that was relayed. I did not take notes but there was much said about "vision" and "strategy." Employees were inevitably referred to with one of two metaphors:

1. "Backbone." We are the backbone of the organization. You know what? I am tired of "backbone," it's childish. Let's call a spine a spine. Do this with me: every time you see "backbone" in print, think "spine." The Spine of America.

2. "Fuel." Several times employees were called the "fuel that keeps this engine [of the company] going" or something like that. This is rather frightening because *fuel* gets *consumed*. I hope at least I am a clean-burning fuel, that does not emit toxic fumes and contribute to the greenhouse effect.

So, to summarize: go team! I am a spine, ready to be shoveled into a furnace! Let's keep this engine going! With spines!

←*October 5*

On Saturday I had to go to my sister-in-law's MBA graduation. I was theoretically happy to help her mark this special occasion and so forth, but it was not a way I would have chosen to spend the whole day. There was a luncheon, and there were photographs, and then there was sitting in a gymnasium listening to speakers make all kinds of tortured analogies about school and life. Lots of sports metaphors. Lots of acronyms. One particularly cheesy speech tried to invoke something called "Life 101," which will be "your hardest class yet," and I briefly considered hurling myself down the stadium stairs to create a ruckus and make him stop, or at least borrowing a pencil to perforate my own eardrum so I would not have to hear it. At one point this guy said, "And this class [meaning Life 101] *never ends!*" Ahem. Maybe you need to retake Biology 101.

⟵ October 7

Today for lunch I had a weird craving so I got some fat-free chocolate pudding from the grocery store across the street and it was vile. I am not sure exactly what made it so vile. Was it the fat-free-ness? Was it just bad commercially produced chock-full-o'-chemicals pudding? Or am I misremembering that chocolate pudding was ever any good in the first place?

The slogan for this pudding was "Tastes Like Someone Loves You." This is a *terrible slogan*. This is the pudding you eat right before you end your lonely, miserable life, because if you were close, if you were sitting in the bathtub with one of those electric turkey-carving knives, getting ready to carve up your wrists and then drop the knife into the water for some bonus electrocution (if you did this on Thanksgiving it would have extra holiday resonance), but you decided to eat a cup of mass-produced pudding as your last act on earth (hey, don't ask me, this is your crazy-ass suicide), and as you peeled back the lid you noticed it said "Tastes Like Somebody Loves You" but they *don't*, your whole life has been a *lie*—those wrists would be carved and that current flowing faster than you could say "suicide stuffing and cranberry sauce." *Fuck you pudding.*

 **October 10**

THOUGHTS ON GIFT-GIVING AND GIFT-RECEIVING

1. I have already detailed the horror that was the Polar-fleece poncho.

2. When I was at my snottiest and most fashion-conscious stage, carefully blackening my eyes every morning and ready to commit hara-kiri rather than wear anything that didn't meet my eclectic but exacting standards (thank god that's over), my grandmother on my father's side came for a rare visit. Occasionally, Nanny would decide to quit smoking super-long mentholated cigarettes and drinking old lady cocktails. These periods of abstinence always seemed to result in her taking up some sort of evil and unnecessary "craft," which she would then inflict on everyone at holiday gift-giving time. On my fourteenth birthday I opened a box that contained a pink sweatshirt, with puffy-paint hearts up and down the sleeves, and the neck had been "enhanced" to include a little crocheted collar. I remember that my mother made it a point to privately tell me how proud she was that instead of immediately projectile vomiting I was able to politely tell Nanny that it was very . . . interesting. Later my friends and I burned it and buried the ashes in an empty field in a sort of made-up goth ceremony. Death to pink puffy paint!

3. A few years ago, LT's father gave us, and then persisted in renewing for us, a subscription to *Mother Earth News*. In case anyone hadn't noticed yet, I live in a large city, have no need to build my own chemical toilet, and am not allowed to keep goats in my apartment.

4. LT has a crazy aunt. I have a crazy aunt too. In fact, I have two crazy aunts, one on each side of the family. I think I have only seen LT's crazy aunt once, but out of courtesy to the crazy we invited her to our wedding, knowing that she would not be able to make it. Six months after the wedding, a box arrived in the mail. Inside was a homemade Xmas tree skirt. It stank horribly of cigarettes. It had a large mustard stain (or something yellow, I didn't want to investigate too closely) prominently in the center. No note was included, and it was only through the postmark (fourth-class U.S. mail) that we were able to figure out it was probably from her. Six months after that, we heard through the family grapevine that the crazy aunt was angry with us because she never received a thank-you note. So I am a bad person for not realizing that something that arrived six months after the fact, in an inappropriate season, with large scary stains on it, and with no note, was a wedding gift. My bad.

5. My own personal crazy aunt (one of them) gave me the same jewelry box two years in a row when I was a kid. The musical kind with the pink plastic ballerina. Exact same jewelry box. The second year, there was a pocketknife inside. I was eight years old.

Honestly, to me, it's all about the giving. Well, not so much about the giving as about the fudge and the mistletoe and the cocktails. But I have never been *upset* about any gift, no matter how horrible, because it is always funny in its own way, and it's not like you were really entitled to anything in the first place. That is why they call it a "gift."

Friday I worked a twelve-hour day, more or less, neglected to eat anything of significance, and then thought I could go out and have four quick beers with colleagues. Not quite. I didn't embarrass myself (unless you count the public admission of a fondness for Fleetwood Mac embarrassing myself) but I did wisely make an abrupt departure at around 10 P.M. before I could make any more mortifying musical revelations, smoke any more Marlboro Reds, or talk more shit about members of upper management. I caught a cab home and had a Gardenburger in front of the television with LT, while watching a nature program called *Rhino!* Did you know that the rhinoceros has the longest sexual staying power of any large mammal? They do it for twenty to thirty minutes at a time. That's not like a marathon or anything, but it's pretty impressive for the animal world. Go rhino! Get busy! Oh yeah!

⟵ *October 13*

There should be government-subsidized Gummi worms. Particularly if you can prove that you Have a Problem. Recently I went for a solid week without feasting on worms, without the help of the patch or anything, yo. I had a few bad moments but then it started to get easier, and I thought, Wow, I'm clean, I am going to beat this thing. But then I went to the drugstore for a few things and there was a package of worms right there at the checkout line and it's like I went into a functional blackout and when I came to I was walking down the street with a green-and-yellow gelatin nematode hanging out of my mouth. Yeah. I'm back on the invertebrates. Somebody do an intervention on me. Or at least make a *Behind the Music*–style documentary on my nightmare descent into Gummi addiction.

◄── *October 16*

This document is getting too long. LT might scoff at calling a hundred-plus pages of typing "long," having suffered through the agonies of writing his dissertation, but this is just a diary and who do I think I am, Marcel Proust? The self-conscious way that we started this diary, this strange exercise, this navel-gazing funhouse mirror of weirdness, might just be the way we (wait, who's *we*? I fell into this vat of words all on my own) end it, with one of those tiny little anecdotes that I claim to hate. You know, the kind that make appearances in the best-selling fiction and, with their charming and imagery-packed prose, tie up the narrative into a neat package and let you close the book feeling satisfied.

My anecdote, unlike those best-sellers, will not featured apple-tree boughs laden with ice, the gnarled hands of wise old grandfathers, or a flock of birds taking flight in the autumn sunset of our ancestral home. It will, however, feature rotting foodstuffs, and although I know it sounds weird, it captures how I feel about Chicago, and how I feel about being thirty years old and acutely feeling the ugliness of the world but also its strange and lovely corners.

A few years ago, LT and I came back from our stint in the Middle East and moved to an apartment in Ravenswood, right by the El tracks. The Ravenswood El line runs up the alleys of Chicago, and lots of apartments and houses back up right next to it. This makes for some interesting window gazing.

There's a place, right before the Belmont stop, where the train slows way way down to make this big curve. One day not long after moving in I noticed a gallon milk jug, about half full, balanced on the railing of a porch on a third-floor apartment. And I noticed it the next day. And the next week. And the next month. Summer turned to fall and the milk level lessened somewhat (perhaps due to evaporation, I never did get close enough to see if the cap was on or not) and turned this marvelous creamy beige color. Fall turned to winter and I was treated to the spectacle of the milk freezing and thawing and, mysteriously, at one point turning entirely black.

It got so I began to position myself on the west side of the train every morning so I could check on the progress of the milk. I started keeping track. The milk had been there around nine months from the time I had first noticed it (and possibly longer than that).

Then, one day, the milk was gone. Just like that. What a

horror show it must have been for the unlucky person who finally went out onto that porch and discovered it.

I found that I missed the milk. It was my friendly decaying signpost every morning on the way to work. Everything falls apart, everything crumbles, everything rots. But everything looks really interesting in the meantime.

Want More?

Turn the page to enter
Avon's Little Black Book —

the dish, the scoop and the
cherry on top from
MIMI SMARTYPANTS

Mimi Speaks!

Hi. Thanks for buying, borrowing, or stealing my book. Every time I mention the existence of this book to someone (which happens more infrequently than you might think), I feel compelled to quickly follow up with the backstories, namely How It Happened, How I Didn't Do It on Purpose, and How Although I Try to Be Graciously Accepting, Much of Me Feels That This Is Insane. And why is that? Why can't I just admit to having written a book? This whole enterprise feels slightly shameful to me, like I am confessing to daily corndog consumption or a bad case of toenail fungus instead of authorship. But enough with the self-analysis, and on to the confession. Hi, my name is Mimi Smartypants and I accidentally wrote a book.

I started keeping an online diary in the fall of 1999. Services like Diaryland and LiveJournal, which are very useful for those of us who are minimally competent (at best) in web design and HTML, were just getting off the ground, and I liked the idea of an anonymous space in which to write whatever the hell I wanted. I've always been a prolific letter writer and e-mailer, but there is a lot to be said for spreading the words around, particularly when you suffer from can't-shut-up-itis like I do. Too often some hapless acquaintance has sent me a "what's up?" e-mail only to receive a two-thousand-word screed on the societal implications of my breakfast or the entertaining antics of crazy hobos on the subway. This is precisely the sort of thing one should vomit up onto the Internet, and not necessarily inflict on one's friends.

God only knows what "popular" means when talking about

something as ephemeral and unnecessary as Online-Land, but I guess the diary became fairly popular. Part of that was undoubtedly due to my diary being one of maybe fifty or so on the whole Diaryland site back in the early days. Gradually I got linked, showed up on other people's "favorites" lists, got lots of "you rock" e-mail. It was an organic process, and I can honestly say that nothing terrible has come of putting my personal stories online (to answer the question that always seems to get asked). My husband learned of the diary and was not chagrined or embarrassed. I did not lose my job. I did not lose any friends. I had only one semiserious stalker, whom I found more entertaining than alarming, and his ardor fizzled out soon enough. As the incredible mundanity of my entries will attest, my life is quite drama-free. The inside of my head is a freaking mess, with daily Manichean battles between good and evil, obsession and acceptance, white-hot anger and glib giggliness, but my actual life = smooth sailing.

(So *How did the diary become a book?* you are screaming. Well I'm *as puzzled as you.* I'm getting to that.)

Anyone capable of stringing two vaguely entertaining sentences together gets told, "You should write a book." I got this comment via e-mail a few times, and I never quite knew what to say. Is it a compliment? Is it a suggestion? My reaction was never, not even for a flicker of a microsecond, "Well, maybe." I didn't want to write a book. That sounded hard. That sounded like trying. I wanted to continue on in my cheerful little no-pressure cyberspace world, where I could type whatever I wanted with very little judgment or consequences, with the added happy accident that a growing number of total strangers seemed to enjoy my babblings.

Then one day I got one of those "you should write a book" e-mails, but from HarperCollins UK. And they didn't even need me to do anything difficult or brain-taxing like *actually write a book,* they just wanted to publish some of my old diary entries in book format. To be honest, I thought this whole proposal was wack. First, my diary is still ongoing, because I am still alive. How would this diary-into-book end? Would our heroine head off into the sunset, having Learned a Little Bit About Life and

Love and so on and so forth, all chick-lit soft-focus until readers everywhere got the dry heaves? Or maybe something really dramatic and action-movie-esque, with a gutshot Mimi Smartypants gasping out one last wisecrack in her garbagey alley? Also, the whole thing just felt like cheating. Many incredibly worthy authors struggle and suffer to get their books published, and many more toil away at brilliant novels in obscurity. I go blah blah during my lunch hour on my happy little subdomain, writing something that is *not a book,* and out of the blue comes a publishing contract. I considered saying no to the whole thing, but when it came down to it I was just not punk rock enough to say no to HarperCollins. Or to their checks.

A few fun data points:

a. I insisted on retaining the pseudonym. It's more fun that way, and I really don't need psycho e-boyfriends hunting me down because of the book.

b. I did not create the cover art or the blurb copy, or have anything to do with developing the book's marketing. Which is a good thing, because bookstore shoppers would probably not be bowled over by "The dead-tree version of some online stuff I wrote."

c. Being published in the UK first, and seeing all your trucks become lorries and your elevators turn into lifts and lots of extraneous *u*'s everywhere, is pretty funny.

d. There was a provision at the very end of my contract that stipulated all the possible spin-offs of this enterprise, and what percentage of the revenue belonged to HarperCollins UK if the spin-offs occurred, and one of the things mentioned was action figures. *Oh please, can we have action figures?*

I know some people don't believe me when I post about how completely underwhelmed I am about the book and the really-very-puny-in-the-scheme-of-things media coverage of my silly website, and these same people assume that a mere scratch of my "eh" surface would reveal a drooling frame-obsessed media whore who jumps up and down like a *Price Is Right* contestant at every link or book press release. You can believe what you like, but *my* "eh" *is sincere.* Think of it this way: you happen to have a drawer full of grocery lists. Grocery lists stretching back to 1999 or so. Some big publishing company comes along and says, "Your grocery lists would make a great book! We could make money off your grocery lists! You could make money off your grocery lists too, although probably not quite as much as us!" You would probably say yes because why the hell not, but you would not suddenly fancy yourself the Jane Austen of grocery lists. You would not quit your job or buy expensive pointy hipster shoes or say, *"Don't you know who I am?"* to the bartenders at the Rainbo. You wouldn't even call yourself a "writer" because dude, grocery lists? Come on. This book thing has been a bit like the log ride at a theme park: I have a feeling I will end up slightly damp, but mildly exhilarated and hopefully not very nauseated.

Plus, it's just plain weird to go back and read old diary entries, as everyone who has kept one knows, and find that earlier version of yourself. It gets exponentially weirder when part of an ongoing diary is pinned down, slapped between covers, printed, and sold. I want to follow readers around saying, "But wait, there's more!" Which I guess is sort of what I'm doing by keeping the online diary going. It also feels very strange to have written a book about my life that doesn't include my daughter, who is such a huge focus of my present-day writing. One of the editors at HarperCollins suggested a sequel, a sort of "Mimi With Child" follow-up to the story, but that sounds like a really bad reason to write a book. "Here, sweetie, you can be in Mommy's *other* book!"

This book, this one right here, has now been published in the U.S. and I get to experience all the surreality of its UK release all over again (minus all those extra *u*'s). Doing something out of character, something that Published Authors do, like writing this back-of-book material for HarperCollins, makes me sort of hover above myself like a camera crane on a movie set. It is not a despairing feeling, just an odd third-person "wow, I guess this is me" feeling. And the feeling has nothing to do with "oh I have gotten so old it seems like just yesterday I was eating three hits of acid and carrying a tire iron around and getting questioned by the cops about it." (Note: true story.) I hate that crap. There is no "magic" age when you are a "grown-up," that's so reductionist and fake and lets millions of slack twenty-somethings off the hook for not doing anything with themselves. Your life is your life! Stumble through it proudly! Weave in and out of the parked cars of your life, shout at the lampposts of your life, puke in the bushes of your life's neighbors!

I realize that my seize-the-(drunken)-day exhortations might sound a bit hollow coming from someone who fell into a book deal ass-backward. And I don't have any "advice" about writing—seriously, if you ever hear anything remotely resembling advice about writing coming from my mouth, hit me over the head with the nearest blunt object. I'm just a girl who likes to type, and who is abnormally desperate to convert some of her internal monologue into the written word. Did you ever see that movie *Speed*? Where the bus will explode if it slows down? I always thought that was a wonderfully convenient way to turn a movie into one giant car chase—you really have to hand it to the people who made that for not even bothering, for just taking a certain stylized trope of action films and stretching it out to two hours. Anyway, that is like what goes on in my world: if I stop typing the bus blows up. Or something like that.

MIMI SMARTYPANTS is the pseudonym of a writer and editor who lives in Chicago. Her ongoing diary can be found at *smartypants.diaryland.com.*

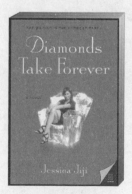